GOLDEN BOY

Valerie Gills

contents

01-Help Me

I thought he was helping me.

I was drunk, drugged and could barely walk straight - no, I could barely walk at all - when bright, police lights flooded my vision. I hadn't knows I was drugged then - how would I? I'd never been drugged before. Isn't it only girls who have to worry about those things?

I remember panicking, the can of beer in my hand sloshing over the opening and dripping down my already alcohol sticky hand. I hissed at the bright lights, wanting nothing more than to either hit the dance floor with my friends or just fall right down there and fucking sleep.

Before I could make my choice though, a thick, meaty hand grabbed mine, pulling me away from the flock of drunk teenagers trying to run out to safety.

Barely coherent words escaped my lips as I was dragged away, my eyes not able to lift from the hairy arm attached to mine as he dragged me upstairs. My feet tumbled over every single step, making me wince when my toes jerked against the hard wood. But I let him take me, because God knew I needed to get out of there, and this man would protect me from the police.

Whoever he was.

I remember trying to ask him for his name, even as I bumped into the walls, even as he took me down to the end of the long hallway and pulled me into a room.

The sound of the lock clicking into place made me snap my head up.

He's just being cautious from the police. Was what I'd thought then.

"H-Hey? Are they gone? Who...Who are you?" I slurred, falling onto the bed and exhaling in the comfort the warm mattress provided me. "Fuck, I need to call Evie."

"We'll be fine." He said, his gruff, deep voice gurgling through me uneasily, and I forced myself to sit up, even though it made my stomach churn.

"Dude, I gotta...get my girlfriend-"

"She's safe."

"Y-Yeah? I better give her a call the-"

"Keep quiet, I think the police are here."

That shut me up. I quietly shuffled to look at the door, finally catching a glimpse of the man. I couldn't make him out perfectly, but I could trace his silhouette. Tall, maybe my height? Old, with a big potbelly and thick, fatty arms. His shirt stretched over his torso, pants barely holding against his biff thighs. He looked like a short sumo wrestler.

I snickered to myself quietly, enjoying my private little joke about how this man would make a perfect sumo wrestler, if he was taller.

"Are they..." I trailed off, and the man stayed silent for a single moment before walking up to me.

In hindsight, I should have run. I should have gotten onto my extremely unsteady legs and tried my best to get out of there, jump out a window or something.

But, no, I didn't, because I was a guy. What could possibly happen to me?

I guess that was my biggest mistake of all. Believing I was invincible because I had an extra set down there. If I had a redo, I would have screamed bloody murder, tried to get the police to me even if it meant getting arrested for underage drinking.

But, I didn't do any of that, because I was never taught to. They never teach the boys, how to deal with this kind of thing. It's never the boys, always the girls.

So when I was held down, forcefully stripped of my clothes against my will, I had no freaking clue on what was happening. By the time I realised what he wanted from me, what he was going to take from me without my permission, without my consent, it was too late. It was too late.

Right now, hours later, when I'm lying on the same bed, in the same room, naked and bruised in ever single nook and cranny of my body, only one thought reverberated through my head.

I was just raped.

02-aftermath

C hapter 2

Aftermath

XOXOXOXOXOX

He left a while ago.

I didn't seen his face, nor do I wish to, as I was certain it would haunt both my dreams and my nightmares.

I didn't know what to do for a long time, just lying there in my filth (I peed myself) and staring at the wall emptily.

I know what a girl should do in this kind of situation. Wear her clothes, don't wash up because the evidence can be used against the rapist, and head down to the police station. Should I do that too?

No way.

Would anyone even believe me? Me, Arryn Donatello, golden boy of Mary Jane International High school, has just been raped by some old fat man in his best friend's house party which he went to almost every single week? Even more, he couldn't remember his face.

I didn't see his face.

But I know I can't stay here any longer, so I force myself to push off the bed and slowly walk to the pile on the floor where he threw my clothes. I wince as I pick up my t-shirt. He'd almost ripped it in two.

Sighing, I slip it over me and grab my jacket to hold it in one piece. Next came my boxers, jeans and finally my belt to click it all into place.

Dusting off my thighs, I painfully look around for my phone, and sigh in relief when I see it lying on the bedside table. It doesn't look cracked or broken, but it isn't switching on. My battery is probably dead.

I avoid all the mirrors in the room the best I can, knowing that I do not want to see myself in this manner. I want to take a bath, so so badly, but my need to get out of this house is greater so I bolt out of the room and walk down the hallway.

I know this house like the back of my hand - I have been coming here to hangout for years now with my best friend, Hale Mirella.

The house seems empty from what I can see. Hale probably crashed at Jason's or Donna's house. His parents are never home, so I don't need to worry about them either.

Making my way through the hall, I walk to the front door and grab the handle, grimacing at the wetness that greets my palm. Pushing the door open, I step out, wiping my palm on my jeans and walking down the steps of the porch. The porch looks how it looks after ever party - cups and booze strewn everywhere, missing pieces of clothing, cigarettes and the occasional drunk idiot. I ignore the guy strewn across the grass and walk to the gate, pushing it open and heading out.

The cool, sharp air of dawn blows across my face, and I make my way over to the house of the only person I know I can trust to see me like this.

It isn't very far, we all live within walking distance of each other at Upper East sector. It's probably how I met my circle, and became friends with them. We were all rich, terribly good looking and absolutely horrible. Aka, popular.

Walking up to the modern suburban house, I go to the side of the house and look up at the window. Grabbing a stone from the ground, I toss it up and smile in satisfaction when it hits the glass pane with a dull thud.

The window opens almost instantly and a blonde head pokes out.

"Rin?!" Her shriek floats down to me, and I manage a half-hearted grin in return. Evette Wilson looks both furious and relieved, and I somehow manage to pull myself up the tree that grew right in front of her window. I don't know what her parents were thinking; it was basically an invite for any boy to climb into her room.

"Hey." I whisper, slipping into the window and landing on the cushioned sill.

"Hey?!" she whisper shouts, closing the window and folding her arms in front of her massive chest. "The fuck, Rin?! I was so worried about you!"

"I'm glad you got out okay." I say, and her glare intensifies.

She switches on the lamp on her night stand, and sucks in a sharp breathe when she turns around to face me again. "Did you get in a fight or something?" she asks, not bothering to keep her voice down anymore as she strides over to me and cups my face with gentle fingers.

I flinch and she retreats her hand, blue eyes dark with worry as she steps back.

"Dude, what happened?" she asks, and I sigh.

"It hurts to be called dude by your own girlfriend, you know?" I tease, and she places her hands on her hips - her no nonsense stance. "Fine." I sigh, trying to come up with a story as quickly as I can. "After the party, when the police came, I didn't know what to do but thankfully someone pulled me out to safety. We went to Blue's Bar, and over there I got more drunk. God knows what happened but I think some guys tried to piss me off or something and I took a swing. It just escalated from there."

"Jesus fucking Christ." she curses, shaking her head in disappointment. "At least tell me you got a good swing in?"

"Yep." I say, and smile slowly when her own lips twitch.

"But you obviously got beat." she says, and I wince when she flicks my forehead. "Ass. Wait here, I'll clean you up."

I diligently wait there, sitting on the soft cushions of her window sill as she disappears in the bathroom to reappear a second later with a first aid kit.

"Remove your jacket." she instructs, and I stiffen. I really don't want to do that, and unconsciously pull it tighter around me. "What?" she snorts, when I didn't moved. "I've seen you in your tighty whities. Don't be shy now."

I guess she is right, we've known each other for a long time, hell, we used to take baths together when we were in primary school. I slowly slip the material off, folding it neatly and keeping it beside me. It is just a piece of clothing, but I suddenly feel naked and just want to curl up on her bed under a comforter.

"Wow, they really did a number on you." she sighs, raising her eyebrows at my torn t-shirt. "Sit still, okay?"

I nodded, and she props herself on the seat beside me before taking a piece of cotton and bringing it to my face. I exhale at the soft feeling of the wet, cold cotton against my bruised cheek, her hand slowly moving to remove the small flecks of blood.

"I waited for you, you know." she says, taking the cotton back and squeezing some sort of cream onto it. "When the police came, Jason and I were standing out in the garden, so it wasn't hard for us to run. But when I met the others, and didn't see you with Hale, I got worried. The rest wanted to leave, Hale was too hammered to even say a coherent word, and they were all saying you'd be fine but I wasn't so sure so I stayed back and waited for the cops to bolt. Once they left I went back in to search for you, but you weren't there. Figures, since you were at Blue's by then."

I feel a sharp tingle erupt at the base on my spine, and it slowly travels up my back and spreads all the way across my shoulders. Evette had come back. She'd been there. Right there, when that man had-

"Arryn?"

"Yeah?" I choke out, and she leans forward to peer up at me. I could count the tiny freckles on her cheeks, her baby blue eyes wide and unblinking, piercing through my soul. I turn away, as if she looks at me for longer she'll figure it out.

"It's done." she says, standing up and closing the first aid box. I lift my hand to feel the soft material of gauze taped onto my cheek, where I was punched almost brutally when I tried to escape. Then, it had felt like my jaw had shattered. But I am grateful that it is only a bad bruise.

"Thanks, Evie." I say, leaning forward to kiss her cheek. Both her parents are doctors, so she's pretty much grown up being around different patients and stuff. They even used to take her and her brother to hospitals whenever they couldn't come home, so Evette picked up some pretty amazing skills in her time there. But it was something only Hale and I knew, as she threatened to filet us if we ever spread the word. According to her, it would ruin her image as a cheerleader. How, I still don't know.

"Go take a shower, yeah? I'll make you some hot chocolate and toast." she orders, standing up and running her fingers through her long, blonde hair. The spaghetti top she was wearing tightly hugs her body, and I stare at her back as she walks out.

"Thanks." I call after her, waiting for her footsteps to disappear down the stairs before standing up and heading to her bathroom. Her bathroom is huge, bigger than even mine - and that's saying something. I love taking showers in her bathroom because she has this automated shower stall which has water massagers and really cool disco lights.

Closing the door, I hesitate for a second before locking it. I never did before, but now I felt the need to. Swallowing, I strip off my shirt, grimacing at it's smell and throwing it into the trash. Doing the same with the rest of my clothes, I finally stand in front of the vanity, completely naked and seeing my body for the first time since yesterday.

Bruises dot my torso, unwanted hickeys splattered over my chest and neck. I feel my lip wobble slightly as I run my fingers over the bite mark low on my collar bone. It's low enough to be covered by my t-shirt, probably why Evie didn't catch it. There is an especially tender spot on my right side, from where he punched me when I tried to kick him in the face. My thighs are a nightmare. Finger prints, slap marks, bruises and bites. He made sure to mark every single inch of skin I had.

Not all of them are shown though.

My legs are relatively fine, and so are my arms. I guess I can cover up the marked places properly with hoodies and jeans. They will probably go away in a couple of days right?

I press my eyes tightly shut, forcing myself to not let the tears fall, and walk to the shower stall, opening the glass door and stepping inside. Putting the settings to what I usually like, I wait for the water to come before closing my eyes against the rush of the warm shower. The droplets dribble down my skin and I feel slightly better, the knot in my throat unwinding. I feel cleaner, not completely but it feels good to have the water wash away the residue left from last night.

Honestly, I can't even feel anything anymore.

At first, it was confusion, anger, disgust, that slowly morphed into horror, fear and absolute terror when he held me down, and I couldn't fight back. But then it all just disappeared, and I couldn't feel anything anymore. The physical pain had ebbed away to a dull throb, and every time his hips moved against mine, every time his burly hands held me down, I slowly started losing focus, slowly started losing the connection I had with reality around me.

Now, all that is left is emptiness and regret. Regret because I couldn't do anything. Regret because I couldn't fight back.

Using her lemongrass shower gel, I clean every nook and cranny of my body, scratching at the skin with fervor to try and get rid of his touch, his marks. But how much ever soap I use, how much ever shampoo I use, the dirty feeling at the pit of my stomach doesn't go away.

Am I always going to feel like this? Like I am a piece of trash lying on the ground? Like if Evie, or Hale, or mum touch me, they will contract some kind of disease, a disease that only I have?

Pressing my nails into my palm, I step out of the cubicle and grab a white towel, slowly rubbing it down my body. When I am completely dry, I wrap it around my chest, like a girl, because I feel way too exposed with it just covering my waist.

I stop at the door, having just unlocked it. I don't want to go outside. I don't want Evie to see me like this, without my clothes there to protect me.

"Rin?"

I gasp and stumble back, heart beating a mile per minute at the shock of hearing her call my name so suddenly.

"Y-Yeah?" I ask, clearing my throat and trying to get my breathing under control as I slowly walk back to the door.

"You done? I've got the hot choco. And the toast."

"Yep. I'm done. Could you, uh, could you pass me my clothes?" I ask, pursing my lips together tightly.

"What? Just come out and take it." she says. I don't blame her. I've been staying over for years now. I already have a quarter of my wardrobe in her cupboard. And I've never bothered to change in private either.

"I...please?" I croak, the heat of humiliation burning my cheeks as I pray to the Gods that she would drop it.

"Alright. One sec." Relief courses through my blood and I wait patiently for her to hand me my clothes. The door swings open and a ball of clothes hits me right in the face. I yelp and catch them as they fall, blinking in shock at Evie.

She grins and closes the door, leaving me alone.

After changing, I look at myself in the mirror once more, making sure everything is covered. I'm grateful that she gave me a full sleeved sweater, along with jeans and boxers. Steeling myself, I run a hand through my toffee blonde hair, pushing the bangs out of my brown eyes and turning around, walking to the bathroom door.

Finally stepping out, I inhale the sweet scent of chocolate and butter toast, thankful to have such a great girlfriend.

"Thanks." I say, sitting down on the bed next to her and grabbing the plate from the small foldable table she kept it on on her bed. "So good." I moan, taking a bite of the toast.

She smiles and nibbles on her own toast, leaning against the pillows.

"You don't seem very hungover." I comment, and she snorts.

"Please. I barely had anything to drink. Remember, I arrived late. Hardly downed a cup before the cops arrived." she explains, handing me a cup of hot cocoa.

"Did they get anyone?" I ask, and she shrugs.

"Not any of our friends." she says. "Hale crashed at Donna's, I think. Jason went back home."

"Sweet." I take a gulp of the delicious concoction. Evie makes the best hot chocolate, second only to mum.

"So, what are you going to do today?" she asks, turning to face me.

Stay in my room and cry my eyes out.

"Just chill at home." I reply. "Maybe play with Mika for a while. He's been bugging me to spend time with him."

"I have a rendezvous with the girls." Evie says. "Apparently there's this new pancake place opening today at the mall."

"Have fun. We'll go some time if it's good."

"Yeah."

I finish my toast and chocolate, placing them on the tray and taking it down to the kitchen, even against Evie's protests.

"I should probably head back home." I call out, walking over to her living room and running my fingers over the back of the couch. "Mum is going to kill me, God."

"Okay. Drop a text when you reach, alright?" she smooths out a tuft of my hair, and I smile down at her.

"Done." She moves forward to kiss my cheek, lingering for a second before pulling back. She is almost as tall as me, fucking 5'11. She's probably one of the tallest girls in school, and has a body to back it up. I'm a very lucky guy.

"See ya." I wave over my shoulder, heading to the door and leaving with one final glance behind me.

My house is only a 5 minute walk from here, less as I usually jog. But my body is in no condition to jog, so I trudge along the pathway silently, scrolling through my phone. I charged it back at Evie's.

I internally grimace at the missed calls I'd gotten. 12 from my mother, 5 from Hale and 10 from Evie. On top of that I have about 50 messages.

Clearing the feed, I quickly text Hale, Donna and Jason that I'm fine, that I'm indeed not dead, like they so nicely put it.

My house comes into view fairly soon and I walk up the grass pathway, heading to the porch and knocking on the door.

A second later it flings open, and a red eyed woman stands there, glaring at me.

"Mum-"

"You, young man, are in so much trouble." Andrea Donatello barks, tugging me in roughly and shutting the door.

"Mu-"

"Where were you? What happened?" she cries, brown hair wild on her head, eyes wide in anger.

"I... I'm sorry. I go drunk at the party and ended up at Blue's." I say, the lie tumbling off like second nature.

She exhales out in frustration, shaking her head.

"Dear God." she mumbles, and then pulls me into a hug. "God, I was so worried about you. I thought something bad had happened or... Thank God you're okay."

Tears jump to my eyes, and I bury my face in her hair, inhaling the smell of mom that brings nothing but safety and warmth.

"Go on up now." she says, pulling back. "Mika was worried too, you know. Actually, I think he was more angry than worried. And don't think this is over, we're going to have a talk soon about this."

Forcing a smile, I let her kiss my cheek before I bound up the staircase to my room.

Shutting the door behind me, I lock it and walk over to my bed. It happens almost slowly, as if time has stopped and every second is an hour.

I fall onto the bed, fingers grasping at the white sheets as I curl my body into a tight little ball, forehead to my knees, and I bury under the blankets, finally let the tears fall.

I finally let myself go.

03-MATH CLASS

C hapter 3

Math Class

XOXOXOXOXOX

I spend almost 90 percent of my time on my bed, but don't get even 5 hours of sleep.

I know my mom's getting worried, so I pushed myself to take Mika to the movies yesterday. It was such an effort, it almost felt like I ran a complete marathon. But Mika's satisfied, and isn't pulling a face anymore, so I guess it's for the good after all.

But for some reason, I find that doing even the littlest of things drags a huge amount of energy from me. I don't bother to go down for meals anymore, telling my mother that I'm not really hungry, or that I've already eaten something beforehand. I know I can't continue like this, but even the smell of food makes me gag. Going to the bathroom? It feels like I'm running a 100 metre sprint.

I don't know why my body feels like it's fresh out of a trash compacter, and the worst part is even though I am perpetually tired, I can't, for the life of me, get a wink of sleep. I may as well be dead.

But today, I know I need to pull myself together, because it's Monday and I have school.

Yay.

Right now it's 6:30 in the morning. I usually wake up at 6, go for a run, take a shower and head down for breakfast by 7:30.

Guess I'm skipping my run today.

I hear mum's footsteps echo as she goes downstairs to prepare breakfast, and take it as my cue to get up. Pushing myself off the mattress, I hiss as the cold air of the morning hit my bare arms and feet as I slide out of my comforter. I always keep the window shut, and even draw the curtains. I have no idea why it's so cold.

Keeping the comforter wrapped around my shoulders, I slowly pad over to my bathroom. I can hear Mika shuffling around in his room, which is right next to mine. Rubbing my arm, I enter the thankfully warm bathroom and stand in front of the sink.

I wince at my appearance, letting the comforter fall to the ground. I have terrible eye bags, which is strange because can you even get eye bags over the course of two days? My cheeks are flushed, it looks like I have a terrible fever. My usually vibrant and bouncy blonde hair is dead and spangly, dropping into my eyes like dead fish. My pyjamas hang off my frame like a rag. Is it possible to lose weight this fast? I don't think so, but I can kind of see my ribs so I guess I'm wrong.

Peeling off the sweaty clothes from my body fully, I stand in front of the vanity only in my boxers and grab the toothbrush. Squeezing toothpaste onto the bristles, I stick the brush into my mouth and brush my teeth. My hands move slowly, lethargically. I can't bring myself to go faster.

I have soccer practice after school today. I need to think of a good excuse to ditch, because the bruises have still not gone and I don't think I can emotionally handle stripping down in a closed room with a bunch of big, burly dudes. The last thing I need is a breakdown while being half naked in a boy's locker room.

After brushing, I remove my boxers and take a long, hot shower. I need to get all the dirt and grime out of my hair, and scrape off all the dried sweat from my body. I think I took almost 12 baths over the course of 2 days, but I somehow always manage to get dirty again. Figures, since I'm nothing but a violated piece of trash.

I freeze when the lights flicker above me. Something moves in my peripheral vision and I gasp, jerking so hard that I slip and bash into the wet wall.

Calm down, idiot. It's just your shadow.

Forcing my breathing back to normal, I rub my left bicep as I right myself, standing back up straight and turning into the shower.

I need to stop getting scared by little things. Soon, people will start noticing.

After my shower, I dry myself down and walk back out to change. I double check that my door and window are locked, but just for insurance keep a baseball bat right next to me. Just incase.

Grabbing my underwear and jeans, I slip them on and go through my messy pile of clothes for a hoodie or a sweat shirt. I usually wear normal t-shirts or tops for school, but now there is no way I'll even step out of my room without full sleeves. I would wear a sweater but it isn't cold enough for that.

Opting for a simple white hoodie with some red gibberish on it, I pull it over and close the doors of my closet. Going over to my desk, I grab all the strewn books and papers that has homework I was supposed to finish, and stuff it in my bag. I'll probably get detention or something, but it's okay. I need 3 for them to contact my parents, and I've only gotten one till now.

Swinging it over my shoulders, I look at the bat and debate on whether I should take it with me or not. If I do, I would probably feel much safer going out. But then all my friends will get suspicious. It'll be hell getting it through my mother itself. Deciding against it, I go to the door and unlock it, keeping the window locked. Don't want to be greeted by some nasty surprise when I get home.

"Mika, Arryn! Come down for breakfast!" I hear mum call and, as always, it was right at 7:30.

"Coming!" I answer, heading to the stairs and smiling at myself when I see Mika a little ahead of me, clambering down and tripping over the last step.

"Clumsy Mika." I tease, slapping his head and walking ahead of him.

"I ain't clumsy!" I hear the brat cry, and sure enough, his head pokes at my side and he catches up to me, glaring.

"Why are you talking like that?" I ask, amused at the weird Boston accent he's taken a liking to.

"Cause this boy in my class speaks like this." Mika says, bobbing up and down so that his curly blonde hair bounces on his head. "He's cool."

"If you're going to speak like that, learn it properly. You sound dumb right now."

"I don't!" he shoots back indignantly, shoving me and rushing forward to go and sit on the kitchen island.

Shaking my head, I head over and slide on the seat next to him.

"Arr, you didn't go for a run today?" Mum asks, keeping down a plate of peanut butter and jelly sandwiches in front of us. "I was surprised to see that you were still asleep when I woke up."

"Yeah, didn't feel like it." I reply, picking up a triangle and swallowing down the sudden turn in my stomach. "Can you pack these for me? I'm not really hungry right now."

"Seriously?" Mum says, turning around in disbelief. "You've been saying that the past 2 days. What's wrong? Are you constipated?"

"No, I'm not constipated!" I try to exclaim, but it comes out as more of a pitiful cry. "I've not been doing much exercise, so I'm not hungry."

"Fine, eat at least a half." she insists, pushing the plate towards me. "And I won't take no for an answer! If you don't eat you'll get gas."

Mika snickers at that, finishing off his sandwich and reaching for another.

"Fine." I grumble, taking a triangle again and biting into it. Even though it is delicious, it tastes like sandpaper to me and I have to force myself to eat the complete half.

"Good, now here, take this." Mum hands me a box, and inside it is two more sandwiches. "Don't waste it, and Arr, please eat properly. It's not healthy to skip meals."

"Yeah yeah, I won't." I assure, kissing her cheek.

"Bye mom! Bye Arr!" I hear Mika scream as he runs down the road to where his school bus stops. I wave and head over to my car, which is parked in front of the house and force a smile back at my mum. She is standing at the threshold and waving, wrapping her sweater tightly over her body. She'll leave for work in an hour or so.

After getting in, I keep my bag on the passenger seat and start the car, pulling my seat belt down and driving onto the road.

The ride to school isn't very long, about 15 minutes by car, and 30 by foot. I probably shouldn't be driving right now, because my eyes feel like fucking stones and my hands are basically dis-attached limbs, but I some how manage to make it safely into the school parking lot. Maneuvering the car between the lanes, I successfully park it and let out a deep breathe.

It's okay. You can do this. Just act normal. Be yourself. Nobody will suspect a thing.

The pep talk doesn't really help me steel my nerves, but I knw if I stay in the car longer I will wind up driving back home. So in one fluid motion, I open the door and slide out of the car, slamming it behind me. I lock it up with the key and start walking towards the school.

No turning back now.

"Yo, Rin!" I tense as Jason runs up to me, clamping a hand on my shoulder and shoving me like usual. It's how we usually greet each other, but today I feel my loose footing stumble and a small yelp leaves my mouth as I trip over the cement and fall.

"Woah, dude you good?" I feel Jason crouch down beside me, stooping over me and my heart stops.

"I-I'm fine." I choke out, trying to move away from his large shadow. "Fuck." I whisper, frustrated and pushing myself up on weak arms, righting myself. "Morning." I say, dusting off my clothes and smiling at Jason.

"Sorry man, guess I was too rough." he says, even though he did what is normal.

"Nah, it's fine. I'm like half asleep." I assure him, walking beside him. His short chocolate hair blows in the wind, and his huge 6'5 frame sways as he walks slowly. He is 5 inches taller than me, the tallest in our team.

"So, what'd you do this weekend." Jason asks. "I took a girl out." he grins, eyes swirling with mischief.

"How was she?" I ask dryly, because Jason never takes a girl out unless he wants to fuck her.

"Great." he chirps, jumping up two steps. "But her sister, on the other hand-"

"Morning!" Jason and I simultaneously turn our heads to see Hale grinning at us from top of the stairs, standing in front of the school entrance with Evie. She has an amused glare on her face, and Donna, who's leaning against the railings, smirks at Jason.

"Jacey, I got 4." she says, and Jason whistles before giving her a high five.

"I got 3. Guess you beat me." he says, shaking his head. "Don, will I ever win?"

"Not while I have a fully functioning vagina." Donna grins, her dark brown hair blowing in the wind as she pushes off the railings. She is dressed typical Donna style; Booty shorts with a blue sleeveless crop top that barely hides anything, and a Mickey mouse bandanna that keeps her bangs out of her face. It went well with her light skin, I suppose.

"You both disgust me." Evie snorts, pushing her hair out of her face. "How do you not get STDs or something?"

"Protection." Donna shrugs, climbing up the last few stairs.

I follow her, feeling a little sick from all this talk about sex.

I haven't had sex before, and neither has Evie. We both want to wait and give it to each other when we graduate. At that thought, I feel a bitter laugh bubble in my throat.

You ain't no virgin now, Arryn.

"Arr, you good?" Evie asks, slinging her arm through mine as we all walk into the school.

"Yeah, peachy." I answer smoothly. Hale comes up on my other side, and gives me a large grin.

"I hit 15k yesterday." he says, and my eyes widen.

"No fucking way." I say in wonder. A little energy enters me at this. "How much time, man?"

"90 minutes." he says, and I have to give him a bump for that.

"That's awesome, I'm still at 12." I sigh. We're talking about the kilometres we can run, and so far Hale and I have been stuck at the 12k mark. But to know that he's hit 15 makes me happy. But it doesn't make me motivated, like it should. I don't think I ever want to run again.

"How much did you run this morning?" Hale asks, swatting away Donna when she starts playing with his blonde hair. His hair is a lighter shade of blonde than mine, mine being more like caramel. He says he doesn't like it because it makes him look more feminine.

"Uh, just 5k." I lie, swallowing down my guilt. "Woke up late."

"Ah." he nods in understanding.

I head to my locker, side eyeing a couple of girls who are whispering, undoubtedly, about me. I can tell from their body language and subtle glances they throw my way when my friends and I walk down the hall.

They immediately stop and turn red, looking away. Evie lets go of my arm, and I hold in a heavy body sag, suddenly feeling even more drained than ever. I know if I really need to, I can go to the nurse's office on some shitty excuse and flirt my way in, or just head back to my car and sleep in the back seat. But I need to stay in school, because I'm not in the right head space to answer all the questions that will inevitably follow, and God forbid I say anything foolish by accident.

Whispers pick up again and I look irritably to my right, where 2 girls and a guy are chatting animatedly about something. I catch my name in the flow, and roll my eyes internally at them. Do nerds think we can't hear them talking about us? We have ears, and you're not necessarily quiet about it.

"Hey, what are you talking about?" Evie snaps, no doubt also getting annoyed by their yammering. "Go and talk your pathetic asses off about us somewhere else, pigs."

The 3 freeze, eyes widening as they all look at each other once and then turn and shuffle away.

"Such losers." Evie scoffs, taking out her biology text book. "Say, you doing anything after school?"

Shit. I know she wants to go out somewhere, and on any other day I would be down. But I'm already feeling like a melted corpse and the only thing getting me going was the thought of sweet sleep after school.

"I...promised to do this thing with Mika." My second lie of the day. "I kind of bailed on him Friday night, so he's pissed about that."

"Oh man really?" she says, shutting her locker and turning to me. "No problem. I wanted to take you to that place I went with the girls remember? On Saturday? It's amazing. Some other time then."

"Some other time." I promise, walking with her to drop her off at her class. Hale joins us on the way, frowning at his phone.

"Dudes, get this." he said, showing us his phone. "Apparently like 8 people got arrested at my party on Friday."

I dig my nails into my palm and force myself to retain a poker face, eyes straight ahead as I pick up my pace, for the first time in my life wanting nothing more than for math class to start.

"No way, 8?!" Evie exclaims, making me silently hiss at her loud voice. "Who?"

"Don't know." Hale shrugs, pocketing his phone. "Someone tried to sue me, ha."

"That never goes down well." Evie huffs, stopping as we reached her biology class. "See you shortie."

Hale frowns, glaring at her as she smirks at him. Hale's the shortest among us, 5'10, and Evie never lets him live it down. He'd been taller than her throughout middle school, but in the first year of high school she shot up like a stalk and is now only an inch shorter than me.

"I'm not short!" he protests, but she ignores him and kisses my cheek.

"See you, Rin." she smiles, turning around and heading into her class.

"Bitch." Hale murmurs, and I nudge him gently.

"That's my girlfriend you're talking about." I chide, and he grins. I know Evie won't take any offence to Hale calling her anything - they are like siblings. But I need to do my due diligence as her boyfriend.

"Bitch bitch bitch bitch bitch bitch." he chants, stopping when his phone rang. "Hello?"

"Motherfucker, you're a bitch, fucking idiot." I hear Evie curse from the other line, and feel my lips twitch.

"Yo-" the line cuts and Hale lets out a noise of frustration. "Fucking hell."

"She knows you too well." I shrug, stopping at the stairway. My classes are upstairs, whereas Evie and Hale have theirs down here.

"See you at break man." Hale waves, walking over to his first period.

I head up to mine, math, and enter the classroom just as the bell rings.

"Hey, Donatello." Peter holds a fist, and I bump it as swiftly as I can. Taking my usual back seat, I stretch out on the chair and feel my muscles sigh in pleasure as they finally get some rest. Pressing my right palm to the left side on my neck, I slowly massage it to get the tension out of the area. God, why is my body aching so badly?

I usually spend math just chatting with my soccer team mates, Peter and Andrew, who sit around me. But today I just want to be that emo kid in the corner and draw my hoodie over my head, fall asleep on the desk.

"Morning, students." Mrs. Marionette, our foreign French mathematics teacher, enters the class. "Open to page 467, let's continue with exercise 7 point 8."

I begrudgingly open my text book to the page, taking out my notebook and flipping to a new sheet. Trigonometry, ugh.

"Now, Memphis, what is sin 3x?" she asks, turning her head to stare at the poor kid in the front of the class.

"Ugh...um..." he stammers, flipping through his notes until he lands on the page. "3 sin x minus 4 sine cube x?"

"Are you asking me or telling me?" she says sternly, and he licks his lips nervously.

"Telling you?"

"Memphis."

"Telling you." he clears his throat, and sits up straighter. "I'm telling you."

"Very good." she nods, quickly jotting it down on the black board. "Now, Serena, tell me the formula for cos 3x."

Class goes on as is, Mrs. Marionette asking us victims whatever questions she can, and leaving the last 30 minutes for finishing the exercise. When she asks me a question, I stare at her until she sighs and shakes her head, mumbling something under her breathe in French. I don't know what it is, but I'm pretty sure I heard the word bête, which from all the middle school French I've learned, I know means stupid.

Well then, thank fucking you Mrs. Marionette.

Earlier, I probably would have cared a little bit, or at least made the effort to text Peter or Andrew for the answer. But today I just don't give a fuck. The true meaning of <I've got no fucks to give> is really hitting me hard right now. I wonder if I'll ever be normal again.

"Don't forget to revise all the formulae, and please, for the love of God, finish the exercise." Mrs. Marionette ends, walking to the desk and removing her reading glasses. "Lea, Kile, Memphis and Arryn stay back. The rest can leave."

You've got to be fucking kidding me.

Everyone collectively gets up, the scraping of chairs and tables resounding loudly through the classroom as the students rush to get out. I gesture to Peter and Andrew to leave without me, slowly standing up and grabbing my books. I wait for the class to thin out before making my way to the front of the class.

Memphis, the first boy to be called on, looks terrified. I don't know why, because he is a standard goody two shoes and I can't imagine what he may have done to get a scolding. Lea is the emo from before. Her black and purple hair is tied up in a weird looking bun, and her face is all white except for the thick mascara and red lipstick she's wearing. She has a lip piercing, and her eyes are dark green. She's wearing cowboy boots that keep clicking on the floor tiles as she crosses her arms in front of her chest.

The last guy is some guy who sits two rows in front of me. I recognise him, because he always gets all the academic awards that are given out at assemblies. Kile Dankworth. That's his name. His black hair is slightly messy, sticking out in a random order. Some fall into his eyes, like mine when I haven't washed it for some time. But his is naturally like that. He wears black glasses, which shield a pair of navy blue eyes.

I look away when he comes over to stand with us, fiddling with his watch. He's wearing a simple hoodie, like me except it's orange, and black jeans.

"Great, all four of you, listen up." Mrs. Marionette says, looking at us coldly. "Memphis, Kile, you both are not in trouble so rest assured."

Memphis almost collapses in on himself, but Kile just smiles, as if he knew from the beginning that he wasn't in trouble. Cocky shit.

"Now, Lea and Arryn." every word she speaks drips with disapproval, and I look down at my feet to avoid her gaze. "It's almost the end of the year. Another 6 months and you'll be graduating. Honestly speaking, with the grades you have, any college you apply to will reject you faster than cup noodles."

Lea snorts at that, and Mrs. Marionette glares at her.

"I know you both want to get in through entrance exams," she continues, "but to get a seat itself to write the exams you must have a particular quota of grades. Frankly, with the grades you're getting now, I'll be surprised if you get into clown college."

"I'll work harder." I say monotonously, as that's what she wants to hear and that's what will get me out of this situation.

"Yeah yeah, I've heard it 10 times by now." she snaps, shaking her head. 'No, this time I will supervise your studies. Now, Memphis, Kile, listen up."

Both their heads perk up, finally being called on.

"You both wanted an final project to work on getting extra credit, right?" she says, and at that moment I feel a sinking pool of dread in my stomach. "Well, here it is. Memphis, Kile, you're the top students in this grade. I want each of you to tutor one of these monkeys, and get them to at least a B+ on the next set of tests."

Memphis gawks at her, and Kile's eyebrows raise to his hairline.

"But-"

"If you succeed," she continues, "I will give you full internals and excellent recommendations to any University you want to apply. I will also personally recommend you to the professors I happen to have contact with."

That shuts them up, and I grit my teeth in refusal, hating this idea to the very core.

"With all due respect-" Lea starts, but Mrs. Marionette shuts her up with a look.

"No ifs, buts, or ands." she says. "Kile, Memphis? Agreed?"

"Agreed." they both say in unison.

"Excellent. Kile, you're with Arryn. Memphis, you take Lea, understood?"

"Mrs-"

"Understood?"

"Yes Mrs. Marionette." I clench out, curling my fists tightly. This is the last thing I need. Especially right now.

I waste no time getting out of there, my heart thudding painfully in my chest as I stumble down the hallway.

Calm down.

I stop and lean against the wall, trying to calm myself down.

Fuck, what is wrong with me?

Anger floods through me at the pathetic state I'm in right now. I hate it. Gods, I hate it.

"Arryn?"

Oh fucking great.

"What?" I snap, turning around.

Kile beams at me and holds up a text book. Running a hand through his ebony hair, he bites down on his full, pink lips and smiles.

"So, when do you want to start?"

04-DOCTOR'S VISIT

Chapter 4

Doctor's visit

"Dude, you got to stop following me around." I say, looking at the nerd in exasperation as I climb down the stairs.

"I just want to know what days you're free after school!" he insists, clambering down after me and holding a notebook in his hands. "Please? I promise to leave as soon as you tell me."

Fucking Hell.

"Fine." I grumble, stopping at the foot of the staircase and glaring at him. "I'm free on Tuesdays and Thursdays after 5."

"Great!" Kile smiles at me, pushing his glasses up his nose. Running a hand through his messy hair, he smiles and writes something down. "Can I have your number?"

"I'm not gay man."

"Arryn." he says, and I sigh before taking my phone out.

"Give me yours. I'll give you a call." I order, and he nods before reciting his digits. Giving him a missed call, I look up at him and raise an eyebrow. He is as tall as me, but since he is standing on a step he's taller.

He smiles and pockets his phone after saving my number, nodding at me. "I'll text you the timings, alright?"

"Okay. Can I go now?" I ask. He nods and bounds past me, probably to get to his next class early.

"Was that Kile Dankworth?" I turn around to see Donna standing behind me, eyebrows raised curiously.

"Yeah. Why?" I ask, and she smirks.

"I took his virginity." she says proudly, and my eyes widen.

"Wait, what?" I sputter, and she laughs.

"Yeah. Summer camp before 11th grade." she smiles wistfully. "Ah, he was good for a newbie."

"You're kidding." I deadpan, because what the fuck.

"Nope. Totally serious." she says, and tugs on my arm to start walking with her. "He's hot as fuck, isn't he? In that genius kind of way. Hot genius. Like Sherlock Holmes."

"Sherlock Holmes is old." I say, and she shrugs

"Bet he was hot in his twenties." she winks, and stops when we reach her class. "Anyways, I think both our parents forced us into that camp to get rid of us for 2 weeks. I was bored and he was prey, so we hooked up."

"Hooked up? As in continuously?" I ask, and she shrugs.

"A couple of times in camp, and a few after school started." she grins, flipping her hair flamboyantly. "I don't know what he did over the summer after camp, but once school started he became amazing. So, so good. Absolutely yummy-"

"Okay okay that's enough." I say, wrinkling my nose. "TMI, Don."

"What's TMI?" And in comes Hale. "Who did you bang this time?" he asks, stretching his arms above his head.

"Nobody except Rin's new tutor." Donna answers, twirling a pen on her fingers. "Kile Dankworth."

"Wait, you mean that Kile Dankworth?" Hale asks. "The one who's currently in the running for valedictorian?"

"What running? Nobody stands a chance against that nerd." Donna snorts. "But yeah. Beginning of last year."

"Holy fuck you're getting tutored? By Kile Dankworth?" Hale snickers, turning to look at me. "R.I.P mate. Have fun spending time with him and those crazy fangirls that follow him around."

"He has fangirls?" I ask, and Donna laughs.

"Yeah. I mean he's pretty popular. Even a few cheerleaders are interested." Donna says. "I think Jenny tried to hit him up a couple of months ago."

"Gross." Hale and I say at the same time. Jenny is a slapstick, annoying raven haired girl who has nothing better to do than chew gum and act like a bimbo. It isn't like she is naturally dumb or anything. She just acts dumb, thinking it makes her adorable or something.

The bell rings, signaling the start of class, and all the students in the hallways begin walking hurriedly to their classes. Someone suddenly brushes against me and I gasp when I see the guy's reflection on the window in front of me.

Fat. Pot belly. Big.

A sort of terror I didn't know I could feel rushes through me and goosebumps erupt on my arms. My breathing accelerates, and every single sound surrounding me becomes distant and more distant until all I can hear is my own heartbeat and ragged breathing. I think Donna is trying to tell me something, but I can barely make out her lips moving and before I know it I am pushing past them, down the corridor and heading for the nearest green door I can find.

Don't scream. Don't scream.

Stumbling into the bathroom, I feel the rats in my stomach go crazy and I hardly stumble into a stall before the triangle of the PBJ I had this morning come rushing out, falling sickeningly into the commode. My shoulders hunch, fingers trembling as they grip onto the white marble of the seat and I force myself to not collapse as another wave of peristalsis hits me and I upturn every single morsel of food and water I've consumed since yesterday.

Shit. Shit. Why now. Why now. I think helplessly, wrapping my arms around myself as I sit back on the floor, mouth disgusting and puke on my nice, white hoodie. Is he out there? Is he?

No he's not. You're being paranoid. How could he be in your school?

But he looked the same. He looked the fucking same.

He just looks the same. It's not him. It wasn't a student. He was wearing a suit. A business suit. He's not a student.

But he's out to get me. He wants to do it again. He wants to do it again. He wants to hold me down again and fu-

"Arryn?! Oh my god." I feel my blood go cold at the voice, lifting my head up to stare through my bleary eyes at... who was that?

"Hey, hey are you alright?" I see a hand coming towards me and jerk away, palms shaking even more as I try to crawl.

Get away from me. Don't come near me.

Stop panicking! Do you want everyone to know you had a breakdown in the middle of school?!

That thought is like a bucket of ice over my head.

"I-I'm fine." I choke out, trying to pull myself up using the wall. "I... had some bad food last night." My vision clears and I see Kile Dankworth looking at me in worry, hands half outstretched as if he doesn't know what to do.

"You really scared me there, Arryn." He sighs, lowering his hands. "I thought you were having a breakdown or something. I was this close to screaming for an ambulance."

Oh thank fuck I got to my senses when I did.

"I wasn't having a breakdown, geez." I laugh bitterly, heading to the sink to clean my mouth and hands. "Shit, I got vomit over my hoodie."

"I can-"

"Rin?" The door bursts open, and Hale and Evie tumble inside. "Holy shit, Rin, are you okay?" Evie stresses, looking scared. "Don told me you just ran away or something-"

"Upset stomach." I say, nodding to the bathroom stall. "I'll go to the nurse and have some medicine. And I need new clothes."

"Man, you scared the crap out of me." Hale breathes, shaking his head. "I got an extra jersey with me. Go to the nurse, I'll bring it there."

"Thanks man." I say honestly, feeling myself get more in control as I stand there. "About soccer-"

"I'll tell coach you're down." Hale waves me off. It is then that they both notice Kile's presence, who is just standing there awkwardly.

"Hey." he says, and Evie's nose scrunches up.

"Who're you?" she asks rudely, and he glances at me before smiling at her.

"I'm Kile. I was in here when Arryn burst in and puked all over." he explains.

"I didn't puke all over." I defend.

"Right sorry." Kile says, smiling apologetically. Does this boy ever stop smiling? "Well, if you're sure you're okay, I'll head out. Have class."

We all silently watch as he leaves the bathroom, slipping out in between Evie and Hale.

"Here, I'll walk you to the nurse." Evie says, as I finish rubbing off vomit the best I can with wet tissues.

"You don't have to." I say, picking up my books which Kile had placed on the sink and following them out the bathroom.

"It's fine. It's on the way to my class anyways." Evie replies, and her fingers brush along my arm in what I assume is comfort, but all it results in was me tugging my clothes around my body harder and stepping a few inches away.

"I'll get that jersey." Hale says, turning around to head to his locker.

I nod at him gratefully, following Evie as she walks down the hallway to the nurse's office. It is at the end of the corridor, and about the size of two classrooms. At one end is a table with a desk for the nurse and a cabinet stocked with medicine. The rest is just beds, each having curtains shielding them.

"Nurse Miranda?" I knock on the door, and she looks up from where she is giving medicine to some kid.

"Arryn? What's wrong?" she asks, gesturing me to come in. "You look pale."

"I had some bad food last night." I say, sitting down on a chair. "I puked, and don't feel so well. Is it alright if I sleep for some time?"

"Of course, but let me measure your temperature first." she said. "Evette, please get the thermometer from there. Arryn, is your stomach hurting?"

"Not anymore." I answer, lying.

"Are you feeling queasy? Does it feel like your stomach is turning?" she asks, handing over a cup of water to the kid for his tablet. He keeps nervously glancing between Evette and I, looking like he'd rather be anywhere but here. I understand. Even I used to feel like that around seniors when I first entered High school.

"A little. I think I need to sleep for some time."

"Okay. I'll give you some medicine to keep down your vomiting. I can't do anything else since you don't have any symptoms." she says, and takes the thermometer from Evie. "Here, put this under your tongue. Wait for the beep."

"Okay." I carry out her order, putting the thermometer under my tongue and clamping my mouth shut.

"Evette, please head back to your class. I've got Arryn from now." Nurse Miranda says sternly, and Evie looks at me. I incline my head to let her know I was okay, and she shrug.

"Cool. I'll come check up on you after this period, okay?" she says, and I nod. She leaves the room, heading to her classroom which is right around the corner.

The thermometer beeps in my mouth and I pull it out, looking at it.

"98.6." I tell her. She checks it and nods, tossing it into the sink to probably clean later.

"Okay, your temperature is normal." she says. "Tim, you should be fine with this. Go lie down for a while, if you're temperature still doesn't go down I'll call your mum to come and pick you up, okay?"

Tim nods, and silently heads to one of the beds.

"Now you." she turns back to me. "Your temperature seems fine, and your tummy is not hurting. You probably have a slight upset stomach, or gas. Are you farting a lot?"

I do a double take at that, feeling my cheeks heat up at her blatant words and piercing stare.

"Not to my knowledge, no." I squeak out, and she nods.

"Okay. I'll give you a tablet to keep down the vomiting. If you're stomach starts hurting again, or if you start getting gas or queasiness, let me know. Do you want me to call your mum?"

"No it's fine. I already told her. She said to let her know if it gets really bad." I lie, and she clicks the back of her pen as she write my name in the medical record. She gets up to get some tablet from the cabinet, and hands it over with a small paper cup with water. I swallow the pink pill and drink the rest of the water, throwing it in the trash when I am done.

"Go sleep." she orders, sitting back down. I nod and get up, ready to head to the bed when Hale enters.

"Hey, sorry- Hi Nurse Miranda." he grins, and she rolls her eyes, waving for him to continue. She's used to us coming in here often, as we get roughed up quite frequently during soccer practice. "I got the jersey. Sorry it took so long, I forgot I'd kept them in the boy's locker room, and spent like 10 minutes searching my outside locker." he apologizes, tossing me the jersey.

"Thanks man." I say, and he gives me a thumbs up.

"No problem dude. Got to miss class."

"Hale, get back right now." Nurse Miranda scolds, and he sticks his tongue out before running back to whatever period he has now.

"I'll just go change." I tell her, and she waves me off. I go to the bathroom attached to the back of the classroom and remove my hoodie, hissing at the cold air that hits my skin. I am still wearing a t-shirt inside, because wearing just a hoodie feels way too thin. Thankfully the vomit hasn't seeped through. Hale's jersey is half sleeved and big for him, so it fits me. I am apprehensive about wearing something that doesn't cover my arms, but I know that nobody will see me sleeping and after this period I can slip out to my car, so I just get down and wear it, sliding it over my already existing t-shirt.

Grabbing my hoodie, I step out and head to the bed in the back corner of the room, making sure all the curtains are drawn before lying down and curling under the thin blanket.

I can't sleep.

I honestly don't know what to do anymore. I am tired. I am lethargic. I can hardly keep my eyes open.

But I can't fall asleep.

My body is fatigued, and I know I won't be able to walk right now even if I try. My head's throbbing and I need to keep taking deep breathes because normal breathing isn't giving me enough air.

I can't sleep. Tim left about 10 minutes ago, and now I can hear Nurse Miranda also leave, probably to take a shit or get something to eat.

I am all alone in here.

I push myself up with difficulty, reaching for my phone which is on top of my hoodie, which is on the floor.

I've been meaning to do this for sometime, but have never found the opportunity to. Someone's always there, or I chicken out last minute.

Well, you're doing it now whether you like it or not.

I switch on my phone and go to my contacts list. After searching for what I need, I grab my hoodie and get up.

Walking to the desk, I take a sheet of paper from the nurse's pad and write down a quick Thank you nurse Miranda. I'm feeling fine now.

I know it isn't much, and that she will notice my absence in school, but I can deal with that later.

Walking out, I head to my locker to get my bag. Evie took my books back to my locker. I smile internally at how she can't help herself from sorting out my usually messy locker.

Grabbing my bag, I open it and take out the extra jacket I got just incase. Thanking past me for his fantastic intelligence, I slip my arms through the holes and zip up the front, completely covering myself up.

Swinging the backpack over my shoulder, I exit the school and head to my car in the school parking lot.

I click it unlock and slide into the driver's seat, keeping my bag next to me. Buckling myself, I reverse out of there and take the road that leads opposite to the one I usually take to get home.

I read about this when I searched it up on the internet, and more than that, it's common sense. God knows what diseases I could have contracted from that guy, especially since he didn't use condoms. I am just glad that I can't get pregnant, or I definitely would be from the number of time he came inside me.

It takes about half an hour, but soon I am pulling up in front of Giselle's World Hospital. Apparently they're pretty good for STD testing.

Parking my car, I grab my bag and phone and walk to the sliding doors. The lobby is pretty big, and air conditioned. I so badly want to cover my face, but it's basically empty and I know nobody I'm acquainted with will be here.

"Good morning sir." The receptionist smiles at me, stopping whatever work she's doing on her computer.

"G-Good morning." I reply, and then clear my throat to get rid of the awful stammer. "I, um, I need to get a test done."

"Test?" she echoes. "What test?"

I'm a high school student standing here in the middle of the morning without my parents on a weekday. What do you think?

"An STD test." I clench out, and she nods, taking out a form from beside her computer.

"Please fill this out." she says, and I take it from her, grabbing a pen provided in a holder. It's all just basic information, and I am thankful that they made name of guardian optional if you're already 18.

"Done." I say, handing it back to her.

"Great, please show me you ID." she requests. I flash her my driver's license.

"Alright. Please go to floor 2, room 171. Doctor George should be with you as soon as he's done with his current patient." she informs me, and I nod.

"Thank you." I say, turning around and heading for the lift.

Riding up to the second floor, I head down the hall until I reach room 171 and sit down on a waiting chair.

It has probably been like 10 minutes, but it feels like hours to me before the door opens and two people step out. One is a female, and she looks to be in her mid thirties. I immediately turn around and flick the hood of my jacket over my head, eyes trained down. I don't recognise her but she might know me.

"Yes, thanks doctor. Yes thanks." I hear her say, before she walks past me and down the corridor.

"Mr. Arryn...Donatello?"

"Yes. That's me." I stand up and push my hood off.

Dr. George smiles at me and turns to his door. His greying hair is slicked back and he has a beard, along with rectangular glasses. He gestures to the door. "Please come in."

I follow him into the room.

05-wrong and right

C hapter 5

Wrong and right

It didn't take much time. Dr. George asked me some basic questions, and I made up some stuff so that it didn't seem too rapey. I told him that yes, I was drunk and didn't remember the guy. But we were both drunk and looking for a hook up so it's fine. But wasn't sure if he used a condom or not, so I just wanted to get tested.

He bought it like a sponge.

It was mostly fine until the physical examination. I think Dr. George could tell I was uncomfortable, because he asked if I would prefer a male nurse instead of a female one. Contrary to what he thought my answer would be, I stuck with the female nurse because I didn't trust myself to be sane while a man saw me without my clothes.

He took a blood test, urine sample and some other stuff that I didn't really pay attention too. I will be called with my results in a couple of days.

That kind of sucks because now I have to wait for a few days wallowing in fear and apprehension, jumping at every call I get.

Right now I am waiting outside the school entrance for Kile. It's already 10 minutes past 6, and he's late (like usual). We have a session scheduled today, and I am still unsure as to where it's going to happen.

"Arryn!" I put on the bitchiest face I can muster and turn to face him.

"Look at that, punctuality at it's finest." I drawl, and Kile winces before stopping and awkwardly rubbing the back of his head.

"I'm so, so sorry." he apologises. "My biology class ran late. I swear I wasn't late on purpose!"

"Okay, fine. I believe you." I say, and bite my lower lip. "How is this going to happen? Are we going to go to a library or-?"

"Oh, we're having it right here, in school." Kile smiles, running his fingers through his black hair to push it out of his face. "Mrs. Marionette got us permission."

"Okay. Which room?" I ask.

"Room 12." he answers, and follows me as I head back in. "So, I was thinking we should start from the beginning of our portions. If we really put our minds to it, I think we can finish most of the stuff by the end of next month."

"Okay. Whatever you want to do." I shrug. It doesn't really matter to me. Honestly, my mind isn't even here, too preoccupied with what my test results will be. Ha, students usually worry about exams, and here I am, worrying about a totally different kind of exam.

"...Arryn? Did you hear anything I said?"

I am snapped out of my trance by his question and I blink at him blankly.

"Uhh, yeah?" I say, and Kile's eyes narrow.

"Try again."

"Yes?"

"Again."

"Please repeat what you said." I say meekly, and he huffs.

"Here I am, putting my heart and soul into this, and you are-"

"I'm sorry."

"-not even interested to hear what I'm saying-"

"I'm sorry."

"It's okay." he grins, and opens the door to room 17. "I was just saying that I have a family pack of Lays in my bag."

"Fucking hell." I glare, and he snorts and walks to one of the large desks. This is, I think, a theatre room, so it's big and spacious with very few desks.

"Did you get your books?" he asks, and I nod before dropping down onto the seat opposite to him, the one farthest so that I don't have to make unnecessary contact.

"Just a few questions." Kile begins, "Do you find some of the basic concepts hard? Like Algebra, trig and stuff? Because there's lots of application from last year into this year's topics."

"I think I'm fine on those." I answer. "Though I was never really good at trig." I continue honestly.

"That's okay." he smiles, and pulls out his own text book. "Nobody is really good at trig."

We start off with the first chapter we learned that year. I, honestly, don't even remember half of it.

Ms. Marionette is a very good teacher, and Kile is really good as well. I understand why she picked him to tutor me. He explains it easily, knows what he's talking about and is able to pick out what I don't understand. Though I find math as a terribly boring subject usually, doing it with him makes it like 2.3% less boring. Doesn't seem like much, but trust me, it is.

I don't know how long the class is supposed to go for, but it's already been 90 minutes when Kile sits back and puts the cap back on his pen.

"I think that's enough for today." he sighs, closing his book. "You're not as bad as I expected you to be."

"Thanks?" I say, and pack my own stuff.

"It's not like you don't understand," Kile continues, "you just don't put the effort to study."

"I guess." I shrug, and take out my wallet. "So, do you charge by the hour, or...?"

"What?" he blinks at me.

"Fees. For the tuition." I explain, and his eyes widen.

"No- No!" he exclaims, raising his hand as if he is being held at gun point. "I'm not gonna charge you, man."

"I'm not going to waste your time for free." I deadpan, and he exhales slowly.

"You're not wasting my time." he says, shaking his head. "This helps me revise too, so I don't need to go home and study. And, I'm getting credit for this. I'm not gonna charge you."

"But-"

"No buts." he says firmly. "I'm not taking money."

"Fine." I relent, sliding my wallet back into the bag. "Thanks though. You know, for helping me."

"No problem dude." Kile gets up, and so do I.

"Where's the emo and Martin?" I ask, as we head out of the room. "Weren't they also supposed to be paired?"

"I think they're doing it on Wednesdays and Fridays." Kile muses. "And it's Memphis."

Figures. They don't look like they have active enough social lives to be busy on Fridays. I think, thanking Kile for holding open the door of the school entrance for me.

"So, Thursday, right?" I ask, and Kile nods. Now that I actually look at him, I wonder how he isn't more popular than he is right now. I mean, he has the looks, the body and the smarts-

Oh right, he is a nerd.

"Yep." Kile confirms. "Got your car?"

"Yeah." I look back at my BMW. "You?"

"Same." he says, glancing at a simple white Impala.

"Well, I'm going to head out." I shift my bag so that it props up higher on my back. I've already gone past my limit of how long I could stay with people constantly, and I really need to head back home and be in the safety of my room again. "See ya later, nerd."

"See ya." Kile smiles and we part ways to go to our cars.

I get in and wait for his car to leave the parking lot before making my way back home.

"Arryn."

"..."

"Arryn! Open your door!"

I sigh as Mika shouts from the other side, placing my Ipad down on the bed and heading to the door to open it.

"What do you want Mika." I say, and the little guy scowls up at me.

"I want to play on the Xbox but it's not loading." he pouts. I sigh and follow him down to the living room. The TV is switched on but the Xbox is failing to load.

"You've not connected to the internet, mate." I say, taking the controller and going to settings. "Mika, I don't believe you couldn't figure this out yourself."

"Now that you're already down, play with me." he cuts me off, sitting down on the carpet and grinning up at me.

I roll my eyes and plop down beside him, giving him one controller.

"What game is this?" I ask, waiting for it to load.

"Star wars Jedi : Fallen order." he replies. "Mum bought it for me last week remember? All my friends are playing it."

"Alright, let's play."

We play for almost 1 and a half hours. I have to admit that I enjoy hanging out with Mika. We're really close for brothers, especially given our age difference. I think we really got close when mum and dad got a divorce around the time Mika was three. Mum always worked a lot, and dad used to take care of us most of the time. Apparently he couldn't take it anymore, and left. I never understood it because I never felt neglected ever in my life. Yeah, my mother did work a lot, but she spent all the rest of her time doting on Mika and I, pampering us. And she got home the money, so I never had anything to complain about.

"Boys, I'm home!" Right on time. I hear the door close and her hopping around as she tries to remove her shoes while standing even though we have a perfectly usable seat in the foyer.

"Is this that Star wars game I bought you last week?" she asks, coming into the living room and dropping her bag onto the sofa. "Arryn, nice to see you out and about and not cooped up in your room like a caterpillar."

I roll my eyes but let her kiss my cheek as she sits down on the sofa between us.

"I tricked him to come down and play with me." Mika tells her proudly.

"Did you-"

"Yes I finished off all my homework!" Mika exclaims, in the midst of a light saber battle with Darth Vader.

I put down my controller and lean back onto the couch, rubbing my eyes tiredly.

"Arryn, how's school going?" Mum questions, leaning forward to look at me. "You hardly talk to me anymore, you know."

"Sorry sorry." I smile, lifting myself up on the couch. "School's fine. Though I've been assigned a tutor for math."

"Tutor?" she looks surprised. "Why?"

"Because I'm failing."

"Dear God!" she cries, eyes wide. "Arryn, you're failing math? Why don't I know about this?"

I shrug.

"You should have told me sooner!" she continues. "I would have set up private teachers-"

"My current teacher is really good." I assure her, purposefully keeping out the fact that he's a student. "I promise I'll get good marks in the next prelims."

"Okay, but if you fail those I'm assigning private teachers." she huffs. Mika finished his game and changed the cord to HDMI 2, so that normal television starts to playing.

"Yes yes." I agree.

I turned back to watch the TV and saw some show playing. I stiffen when two guys kiss on the lips, and suddenly the TV switches off.

"Mom!" Mika protests, and she shakes her head.

"Don't watch shows like that." she snaps, keeping the remote out of his reach. "It's not correct."

"What's not correct?" Mika asks, looking confused.

"Two boys shouldn't kiss on the lips." Mum says sternly, standing up and adjusting her blazer. "It's wrong, okay Mika? You shouldn't do it."

"But why?" Mika asks. "Is it only boys?"

"It's not natural. It goes against nature." Mum explains. "It's not only boys. Nobody should kiss the same gender."

"Okay." Mika shrugs.

"Arryn?" she looks at me.

"It's disgusting. I would never do that." I say a bit more harshly than I meant for it to come. She looks taken aback, but gives a sharp nod.

"What do you want for dinner?" she asks, changing the topic to a lighter one. "Burgers?"

"I want burgers!" Mika shouts, clambering up and following her to the kitchen.

I stay where I was on the couch, silently looking at the black TV screen in front of me.

It's not natural. It goes against nature.

I slide a hand over my thighs, and feel a hot course of anger shoot through me. She is right. It isn't natural. It is abnormal. Wrong. It is obvious from how wrecked my body had gotten after that night. After he had...

I have bruises, I still do, it hasn't gone completely. It hurt to pee and take a shit the day after. There was blood when he was done. So much blood.

No, people of the same gender being together is wrong. They shouldn't kiss, they shouldn't date and most of all they shouldn't have sex.

It brings nothing but pain.

Standing up, I head back upstairs to my room, mood killed and hands shaking as I am assaulted with the memory again.

I know it has been only 4 days. I know that something like this is difficult to get over. But why does it always have to come back? Why does it play in my head like a bad movie on repeat? Why does it always make me so afraid even though I know I am perfectly safe?

Locking the door behind me, I double check if the window is locked before burying into my bed. This is habitual now. Go to school, somehow get through 7 hours, come back home and just stay under my blanket for the rest of the day.

I used to love being me. I used to love being Arryn Donatello, the Arryn Donatello. I was known by everyone in this area, by everyone in the school. Wherever I went, people talked and I thrived in the attention. I liked being popular, I liked being noticed.

But now, I wish people wouldn't look at me. I wish people would just mind their own business. I wish it didn't feel like every single move of mine is being watched, and that he is one of them. He is watching me, among the crowd somewhere. I don't know who he is, I didn't know what his face looks like. I don't even know if he is someone I know. I know a lot of fat people. But I don't, and it feels like he has the advantage. That me being in the dark about him gives him the upper hand, that whenever I am walking with my friends, or sitting in class, or doing math with Kile, he could just jump out and pin me down. That he could do it in broad daylight and nobody would notice. Even if they did the only thing registering through their minds would be Arryn Donatello is a fag.

Sniffling into my pillow, I turn my head to look at the cloudy sky outside the window.

I'm not a fag. I'm not. Just because I was forced to... doesn't mean I'm a fag. It doesn't mean that I am gay. It doesn't. It doesn't.

Right?

I doesn't.

06-math worksheet

C hapter 6

Math worksheet

The next two days go by quickly, and I am relieved when I finally get a call from the hospital on Thursday at lunch.

"Hello?" I spoke, excusing myself from our table and walking over to the door with quick strides.

"Arryn Donatello?" I hear Dr. George's cheery voice on the other end of the line.

"Yes. How are you doing?" I ask politely.

"Great great. All well with you?"

"Yeah, I'm good."

"You must've been eagerly waiting for these, eh?" I hear him chuckle.

You have no idea. I think, as I walk down the hallway to the end and made sure nobody is around. "So, did you get the results?"

"Yes, I did. No need to worry about anything, Arryn. You're free of any STDs. We've done a thorough check up, and the only test we're waiting for is the HIV one, which should be done by this weekend. But the chances seem pretty minimal so I wouldn't be too worried."

"Oh thank god."

"You can rest peacefully now. But remember, next time use a condom okay? Safe sex is the best sex."

"Yes Dr. George." I shuffle uncomfortably, feeling my cheeks heat up. "I'll keep that in mind."

"Oh and another thing, do you think you could come down to the hospital next week whenever you're free?"

My heart skips a beat at that.

"Why? Is anything wrong or-"

"No no! Nothing! You just need to pick up some documentation and bills, that's all. The receptionist told me to inform you."

"Alright. Of course. I can come Wednesday evening, if that's okay." I offer.

"Around 5?"

"Yes I can make it."

"Excellent." I hear a little shuffling about and then he clears his throat. "Alright. I'll see you next Wednesday then, okay?"

"Yep. Bye, and thanks again for everything."

"Your welcome, son." He says warmly, and we cut the call.

Pocketing my phone, I go back to the cafeteria, walking towards my table and sliding into the seat next to Evie.

"What was that call about?" she asks, leaning towards me and lowering her voice. "Are you in some sort of drug business that I don't know about?"

"What? No." I snort, taking my apple juice tetra pack and sipping on it. "It was my mum. She just told me that she'd be late and that I would have to cook dinner."

"Ah." she nods. "Hey, if Mika and you are free tonight, why don't Laurent and I come over? We can order in pizza and stuff and watch a movie or something."

"Sure." I automatically agree, and then immediately regret it. My mum is, in fact, going to be home very much on time and Evie would know that I lied. "How about we come to your place?" I ask. "Mika misses your jacuzzi."

"Fine with me." Evie shrugs. "7?"

"Yea- no wait, I have that tuition thing with Kile. 8:30?"

"Done." she smiled, and steals a fry from my plate.

"Hey!" I protest, and she winks before stealing another.

Honestly speaking, I know it will be a bit difficult for me to stay with people till late in the night. I get really tired at very random moments of the day. And God knows what I'll do if I have a mini panic attack or episode at her house. I just have to suck it up, though, because I already said yes and I can't hide out forever.

After last period, I go to the theatre room where I have my math class.

"Hey." I greet, closing the door behind me. He is already seated at our usual table. Even though there are 4 other desks in the room, we always choose that one for some reason.

"Hey what's up." he says, looking up from where he was reading his math textbook. "You seem tired."

"I just had a very long day." I sigh, sitting on the opposite end of the table and sliding my bag off my shoulder.

"Did you skip practice again today?" he asks, and I am fairly surprised that he knows about that.

"Uh yeah, how did you know?" I ask. I take out my notebook and calculator, placing them in front of me.

"I was there in the locker room when you were talking to the coach." he shrugs, running a hand through his hair. "Upset stomach?"

"Yeah." I feel a little guilty for lying. "I ate something bad on Sunday. I haven't been to practice all week."

"That sucks." he cocks his head. "So, you visited the doctor?"

"Yeah." I told coach that I had, and if he already knows there's no point lying even further. "I did."

"That's good." he nods. "Did he prescribe those fries and burger you had for lunch or was it something you read online?" he smirks.

"Wha-" I feel my jaw open, and my cheeks suddenly become heated coal as I meet his amused eyes. "What?" I repeat, keeping my voice under control.

"Hey I'm not judging. I don't really care if you skip practice. Nothing to me."

"I'm not skipping practice." I say coldly, feeling irritation seep in at that comment. That burger and fries I took was for appearances, because I usually eat quite a lot. If he looked properly, he would have noticed Hale and Evie taking almost all my fries. And I barely had two bites of the burger before I felt like puking. I had to throw it out.

"I'm sorry man, I didn't mean to get you angry." he immediately apologises. "I was just kidding around."

"Well don't." I snap. I already have to deal with enough bullshit in my life. I don't need some nerd to add on to my list of worries. "Can we just do the math already?"

"Yeah sure." he says quietly, not meeting my eye as he flips open to the exercise we'd been doing last time.

I feel a bit bad, but it doesn't bother me very much. It's okay if he doesn't like me. I don't need anymore friends. Managing the ones I already have is exhausting enough.

The whole duration of the class is silent and awkward. Kile hardly looks me in the eye, and answers my questions curtly and to the point. It bothers me after a while, and I want to apologise, but it feels like my throat has clogged and I can't get the words out.

After the painfully slow 90 minutes, I quickly pack my bag and stand up.

"Um thanks for the class." I mumble, feeling a bit shameful. "I should get going now."

"Okay bye." he says, smiling up at me warmly.

I am even more embarrassed for my behaviour, so I do the only logical thing my emotionally unstable brain can think of; I turn tail and run.

I don't really run, but I speed walk all the way out of school and down the lot to my car. Getting in, I throw my bag on the passenger seat and lean forward until my head is resting on the wheel.

Tears had well in my eyes, and I can feel my nose blocking as I sniffle and squeeze my eyes shut. Gosh, why am I so affected? It is such a little thing and I'm reacting so much.

Wiping my eyes on my sleeves, I start up the ignition and put my seatbelt on before driving out. I can see Kile exiting the building just as I pull out completely.

When I get home, it's Mika who greets me.

"Hey Mi." I walk inside and hop around as I try to take my shoes off.

"Can we watch a movie?" he asks, walking with me into the house. "Pretty please?"

"Mika, how would you like to go to Evie's house tonight?" I ask instead.

His eyes widen and a smile breaks out on his face. "Yes yes I want to go!" he cheers. "Let's go now!"

If only I had the same enthusiasm for meeting people. I think dryly as I walk up to my room, Mika trailing behind me the whole time.

"I'll let mom know then. She won't have to make dinner for us." I tell him, tossing my bag onto the carpet and falling onto the bed. Getting my phone, I open my messages.

Mom

07:56 pm

Mooom, Milk and I are going to Evie's tonight.

Don't make dinner for us ok?

Excuse me?

With whose permission are you going?

...

With yours?

Nope, you don't have my permission young man.

You're grounded for this month if you've forgotten.

Moom, pleasee

Are u serious rn?

I'm completely serious.

Which, apparently, is something you lack for your studies.

Ugh

Yes ugh.

You better be home when I get back.

Fine fine. I won't go.

By the way, I'll be back home late today. I have to stay back with a client. Will you be alright on your own?

Yes yes I'll be fine dw

Exhaling I put down my phone. I look over at Mika, who is looking expectantly at me. Guess I didn't lie to Evie after all.

"Mum said no kiddo." I tell him, trying to look sad.

"What? Why?" he whines. "I wanna go!"

"Well you can't." I pick up my phone to message Evie about the news.

❣Evie❣

Ugh my mum said I can't come over cause I'm grounded for a month.

:(

What? Aw that suckss

It's fine, tho. I understand.

Mika's really bummed he can't come tho :/

Then send him over

fr?

Yeah. Why not?

We'll still order pizza and go for a dip in the jacuzzi.

Or we'll pop down to Hale's to use his pool

That sound so fun

Ikr

Ur horrible

ik

Send him over. He can walk to my house right?

Yeah okay. I already told him. He's even happier now that I'm not coming

He gets me

I think he has a crush on you

awww really?

That's so sweet.

Looks like I have competition.

I laugh as Mika snatches the phone from my hands, face red.

"Arryn!" he screams, looking like he was about to cry. "I don't have a crush on her!"

"Sure kiddo." I smirk, and tackle him into a hug. "Now go on, get ready. Tell me when you're heading down to her place."

Mika bounces out of the room, with a little extra skip in his step. I chuckle as I hear him singing.

Standing up, I go to the bathroom to get changed into more comfortable clothes.

I choose a gorilla printed pyjama set which mum got for me from abroad on one of her business trips. I totally hated it but once I put it on, man it felt like clouds on your skin.

Washing up and changing, I step out to see Mika dressed in jeans and one of his nicest tops.

"You're dressed fancy. I smirk. "Dressed to impress."

Mika blushes and then spits, "Well, I'm leaving now!"

"Message me when you get there!" I call after him, waiting to hear the front door close before sagging back into my bed. It feels nice to tease Mika. My life has been so disproportioned for the past week, and I'm barely holding it in together. But having some semblance of normalcy back is like a sip of nectar.

I close my eyes, turning onto my side. I'm home alone. If mom is staying back that means she won't be home at least for another hour, if not more.

I suddenly feel a chill go through me as the eerie silence of the house seeps through. I can feel eyes on me, as if someone is watching me. It's so quiet. I never wondered this before, but if I scream form in here would anybody hear? Or would I be left alone? Pushing myself up, I look around in panic, wondering if- imagining if-

My phone ringing disturbs my thoughts, and I let out a cry as I jump in shock. My heart is racing a mile per minute and it takes me five rings to completely calm myself down.

"H-Hello?" I answer, pressing my trembling fingers into a fist and biting my lip hard.

Calm the fuck down.

"Hey, Arryn. This is Kile!"

"Kile? Oh, hey Kile."

"Are you okay? You sound a bit spooked."

"Yeah sorry. I'm home alone and the phone ringing startled me." I don't know why I told him that, but it just slipped out. I don't regret it.

"Oh okay, never mind then. Are you busy right now?"

"Nope. I'm just lying down. I don't have anything to do." I reply, falling back down and adjusting the pillow under my head.

"Okay great. So let's do some math worksheets." his voice floats through the speakers cheerily, and I wrinkle my nose.

"What?" I said. "I don't want to do math worksheets."

"You do want to pass right?"

"Yeah."

"Then you need to practice. It's only like 5 questions."

"But I don't want to."

"It will take you 10 minutes. If you don't review once you come back home, you'll forget everything you learned that day."

"But Kile-"

"Arryn."

"Ugh fine."

"Great! I've already sent them to you."

"You're such a pain in the ass." I mumble, walking over to my desk and pulling my bag with me. "So, are these hard?" I ask, opening the document on my computer. "Crap, these look hard."

"They're not. Read the questions properly. Text me when you finish them okay? Like I said, shouldn't take you more than like 10 minutes."

"Wait!" I say immediately. "Do you- Can you stay on call?" I ask hesitantly. I feel like a baby asking, but one look at the empty house around me and I decide that having Kile on call just incase isn't so bad after all.

"You want me to stay on call?" he sounds surprised. "Why? Is there some question you don't get?"

"Uh yes." I reply hastily.

"Which one?"

"Question one?" I squeak, feeling myself blush. I'm thankful that this is over the phone, other wise he would see my red cheeks.

"Okay. How about I solve this worksheet with you, and you can solve another one on your own over the weekend?" he suggests.

"Yes please." I say meekly.

He slowly starts explaining how to do the problems. And even though I know how to solve all of them, I still don't tell him and let him explain. Something about his voice is soothing, and I find myself asking questions here and there just so that he doesn't go faster.

I don't even realise over an hour has passed before I hear the door open and mom call out that she is home.

"...and now that we've got rid of the complex denominator, we can just directly substitute the values and get the answer." he finishes, and I copy it down.

"Thanks so much." I sigh, closing my notebook and rustling my hair out of my eyes.

"No problem. I'll send one over the weekend, just like this one. Solve that one too okay? It should help you understand the topic completely."

"Got it." There was a little silence, before I gathered up all my courage and said,

"Hey Kile?"

"Yeah?"

"I'm sorry about before."

"..."

"..."

"It's perfectly alright, Arryn."

07-Soccer Practice

Chapter 7

Soccer Practice______________________

Hey, I won't be coming to school today :((I'm on my period xx

I read the text from Evie, getting out of my car and closing the door.

Oh shit. Rest loads and I'll try to drop by with some ice cream after school. I text back, walking slowly to the school entrance.

It's okayy. Ik you have practice too. It's your first day after a week ^o^ Concentrate on that, okay?

I hesitate, but then reply, Alright :(Gwss

Pocketing my phone, I walk up the steps and am surprised to see Kile waiting on top.

"Hey what's up." he says, noticing me.

"Morning. Are you waiting for someone?" I ask, stopping and looking at him curiously.

"Yeah. You." he grins, and pushes his black hair out of his eyes. "I
thought I'd start this bleary Monday morning with some good news
for you."

"Yeah? What is it?" I ask, and walk to the door, letting him follow me.

"You got all the questions right on the worksheet!" he exclaims,
bouncing next to me and beaming with happiness? Pride? I can't tell.

"No way, for real?" I say, and snatch his phone when he holds it out
to me. Pictures of my test with poorly drawn ticks glared at me from
the screen, and I can't stop the small smile that twitches over my lips.
"Wow, I was sure I got like 4 of them wrong."

"Nope, all good." Kile pips, taking his phone back.

"Thanks, it's because of your help." I meant it.

Stopping in front of my locker, I open the lock while Kile leans on
the locker right next to mine.

"You're going back to practice again starting today, right?" he asks.

"Yeah." I nod. "How did you know?"

"You know Gary right?"

"Yeah." He is part of the team, a mid-fielder. He's an excellent player. I think he's already been offered scholarships by many universities.

"Well he's kind of a family friend. he was over this weekend, and he mentioned it." Kile shrugs.

"I didn't know that." I muse, taking my Accounts text book out and shutting the door. "What class do you have now?"

"Comp science." he answers, following me again when I start walking to the stairs.

"Isn't that down here?" I ask, wondering why he was following me up. I'm pretty sure the labs are down here.

"I... need to pick something up from the Math class." Kile sputters, cheeks darkening slightly. "I left my water bottle on Friday. By accident."

"Ah." I resume my walk back up. "Is it-"

I am interrupted by a loud call of my name, and rol my eyes internally, bracing myself as Hale barrels down the hall and crashes into me.

I wince and stumble slightly, catching him against me.

"I need the accounts homework like right now!" he pants, gazing up at me in desperation. "Please? Please? Now! Agh, Mr. Turas is going to fucking kill me."

"Calm down." I urge, gently pushing him off me instead of vaulting him away because I haven't been in this close contact with anyone except Mika and it still unnerves me.

"Give me the homework!" he cries. "I need it right now!"

"Okay okay." I sigh, holding a hand up to make him stop and sling my bag to the front so that I coan open the zipper and fish out my accounts note book. "I need it back when class starts."

"Yeah yeah!" he dismisses, running past Kile and I to the accounts room. I catch, from the corner of my eye, Kile looking after him in amusement.

"He's always like this." I say, and he turns back to me.

"I know." When I raise an eyebrow he chuckles. "What? You and your group are like the poster kids of this school. Everyone knows you guys."

"Says Mr. I'm-the-hottest-nerd-around-and-have-a-groupie-of-fan-girls-up-my-ass." I snort.

Kile's mouth falls open, and he looks so scandalized that I can't help a tiny grin.

"That- that is not true!" he protests, and I shake my head as I walk past him to my class. "Arryn, that's not true."

"Sure."

"I'm not kidding! That is not true."

"And I believe you." I say in the most disbelieving tone I can muster.

"Arry-"

"Well, that's the bell." I snicker silently. "I better get going."

"Wait listen to me-"

"Oh look." I interrupt, and he stops before following my gaze. "Isn't that girl one of your fans?"

"You-"

"Mr. Dankworth, please get to your own class." Mr. Turas says sternly, tilting his bald head to look up at the dude. "It's past time."

"I know right. Mr. Turas, he's kept me past time. He's not letting me enter the class." I say in mock distress.

"I-" Kile cuts off and glares at me over Mr. Turas' head. This is not over. he mouths, and I roll my eyes before turning my back to him.

After Accounts, I realise I have Math and huff a silent laugh about today's morning as I head to my locker.

"...and then her killed the rat!" Hale finishes his story, hands dropping from the air for a flourish. "Can you believe it?"

"No." I say. "How shocking."

"I know right?!" Hale exclaims. "To think the Barbie would be so stupid."

"I know right."

"Aha!" he yells, and I flinch involuntarily at the loud sound. Taking a step back, I discreetly swallow down the flash of panic I felt for a second there.

"I knew you were not listening!" he accuses, pointing a finger at me. "There was no Barbie in my story! It was Mickey mouse!"

"It's rude to point." I reply, walking the rest of the way to my locker. "I'm sorry, but the story was just so terribly boring."

"You know what you are?" Hale huffs, crossing his arms in front of his chest. "You're mean. That's what you are."

"How insulting." I deadpan, shoving my accounts text book in and shutting the locker closed.

"Son of a bitch. Nobody listens to me." Hale whines, as we go back up for my math class.

"Hale you have physics, which is downstairs." I tell him, stopping in my tracks. "Go on now. I promise I'll listen to your Donald duck story in lunch."

"Mickey Mouse!" he hollers after me.

Stepping into the classroom, my eyebrows raise slightly when I take in the slightly empty class, and the occupant of the seat next to mine.

"Dankworth." I say, plopping down on my seat. He turns and smirks at me, leaning on one arm.

"New seating arrangement?" I continue, taking out my stuff from my bag.

"Why? Scared?" he taunts, and I snigger slightly. This guy never fails to amuse me.

"Janet Heavens used to sit there." I point out. "Isn't she one of your alleged fangirls? Did you use your masculine wiles to seduce her out of-"

"Dear god." he groans, cheeks pink as he turns away and covers his eyes with his palm. "You're persistent."

"I've been called worse." I retort. It feels nice, jabbering like this. With Donna, Jason and even Hale and Evie, I feel this sort of pressure to keep up certain appearances. I mean, I have to act like the old version of me, which died along with my innocence that night. But nobody knows about it except for me, and I'm hellbent on keeping it that way. But with Kile, since we aren't even friends, I don't really have to be me in front of him. I can just be... me.

That doesn't make any sense but whatever.

Obviously I can't be completely transparent, but I don't feel as pressured like usual.

"What are you thinking about?" Kile asks, and I pull out of my depressing thoughts to look at him.

"Uh, nothing." I say. "I just don't like math."

"I get that." he agrees. His eyes flit up as a shadow looms over us, and I snap my head up in quick succession to see Peter grinning at me.

"Yo." he holds out a fist for me to bump. I do the due diligence, and peer up at him.

"Heard you're getting tutored by some nerd?" he says, sitting down in his seat.

"Yeah." I sigh.

"Said nerd here." Kile raises his hand, and Peter looks up at him in surprise.

"You're..." his brows furrow and he tilts his head. "Ah...Kale Spinach."

"What?" Kile says, and I just blink amusedly at the two.

"Its Kile Dankworth." Kile corrects disbelievingly. "I get Kale. But why spinach?"

"Cause like... I didn't know your last name so I just went with the first thing that came to mind after Kale." he shrug.

"Rude." Kile snorts. "I can see why you're a below average student."

"Hey!" Peter protests, and then sags. "Yeah." he pipes up again. "But, I've already gotten a free ride to my top choice through soccer, so I just need to pass these exams."

They look like they're going to say more, but everyone falls silent when Mrs. Marionette enters the classroom.

Nothing much happens in math. Kile helps me in some of the sums, forcing me to solve them instead of just lazily staring at a wall like I usually do.

After Math, I excuse myself and go up to the third floor. Entering a bathroom, I close and lock the door just for extra measure. Nobody ever comes to these bathrooms, because only the AV rooms are here, and the clubs meets after school only.

Putting my backpack on the counter, I slowly remove my jacket and the full sleeved t-shirt underneath. I hum approvingly at the slightly less bruised skin.

On Saturday, I realised that none of the bruises inflicted on my body were fading as fast as I hoped. Then it struck me that I hadn't even put any medicine except for a little ice in the beginning and my usual cream. So I went to the pharmacy and bought some gel for it. Whatever it is, it seems to be working because the ones on my upper arm and stomach are fading. The ones on my chest and collar though, will probably take some time.

The packet says to apply it thrice a day for maximum effect, so I apply it in the morning, afternoon and night. But I know that I wouldn't be able to slip out everyday during lunch from my friends without coming off as suspicious, so I have to do it during break. It's only one period more anyway till lunch.

After applying it, I put my t-shirt back on, grimacing at the way the cloth stuck to my abdomen. Sliding my jacket over that, I pack everything up before smoothing down everything so that I look good. Normal.

Gosh, with all this planning and sneaking around I'm doing, I would rock at being a detective or something.

Unlocking the door, I slowly open it and peer out just incase, before hopping out and going down the stairs.

Thankfully I don't meet anyone until I am at my next class, Business studies, which I share with Hale.

"Hey." I greet, sitting down on the seat next to his, at the back like I always do.

"Where were you?" Hale asks, fiddling with his pencil.

"I, uh, had to get something from my car." At this point I am basically a professional liar.

"What did you have to get?" he pries. Such a nosy person.

"My text book." I say.

"Ohh." he nods, balancing the pencil on his nose now. It drops and the girl sitting in front of us giggles.

"You almost held it for a minute." she laughs, and Hale grins.

"I know right?" She blushes when he answers back, and takes that as an invitation to turn around and face us.

"I can balance it on my upper lip." she smiles, pressing her lips together. "By the way, I love your shirt. It's really cute."

"I know." Hale says. "I like your..." he trials off weirdly and looks her up and down, "glasses."

"I'm not wearing glasses." she says, looking confused.

"Well you should." he points out.

"Really?" she giggles again, and twirls a strand of her dark brown hair around a finger. Her eyes flit to me, and she bites her lip and smiles shyly. "Hi Arryn."

"Hey." I reply, not in the mood to talk to anyone. I don't even know her name, to be honest.

"Do you know anyone who looks good in glasses?" she asks, leaning forward so that I can see into her top. I hold in a heavy sigh and avert my gaze.

She looks at me intensely, waiting for an answer. When I replay the question in my head, my mind for some reason jumps to Kile. I guess he pulls off glasses. Quite well actually.

"Yeah I do." I nod. The teacher enters, and I softly use the tip of my finger to press against her shoulder and push her back so that she isn't flashing everybody in the last row. I can see a guy sitting on the other side of Hale who's eyes haven't strayed from her body for even a second. When I look at Hale though, he is staring too but there's a glint in his eyes I can't make out. It's almost as if he is... sad to be looking at her boobs.

"Ooh, time to pay attention!" she giggles, turning back around and tucking a strand of hair behind her ear.

"You good dude?" I ask, still bent on his strange expression.

"Huh? Oh yeah." he straightens himself out and grins at me, though I can tell it is forced. I've been forcing smiles for over a week now.

After class, I try talking to Hale but he dodges every question I ask and escapes before I can interrogate him properly. Making a mental note to ask him about it later, I round the corner to the cafeteria, and bump into someone.

I gasp and stumble back, almost falling on my ass but someone catches my arm and hauls me back up. I'm now crashing forward and my face collides with a chest.

"Oomph!" I groan, clutching my forehead and stepping back.

"Oh God, I'm so sorry." A familiar voice says, and I stifled a sigh. I seem to be sighing a lot these days.

"Kile, how do you always manage to cause trouble for me?" I say dryly, stepping back as Kile bites the inside of his cheek guiltily and smiles.

"Sorry." he groans, tipping his head back. "I'm so clumsy, it's a wonder I haven't broken 5 toes till now."

"Keep this up and I'll break them for you." I start walking in the direction of the cafeteria. He, as always, follows right behind.

"I'm so hungry? Are you hungry?" he asks.

"Not really." I say truthfully. "But don't tell my mum."

Kile chuckles, and I feel my eyebrows raise in surprise as I turn to look at him.

"What?" he asks, looking sheepish all of a sudden.

"Your voice. It was so deep then." I comment.

Kile's cheeks pinken and he looks away. I stare in amusement at him, leaning forward to catch his eye.

"Do you do it on purpose?" I ask. "Do you actually make your voice high intentionally?"

"Stop it!" he whines, trying his best to not meet my eyes but keeps failing. "It's just a habit."

"What sort of weird habit is that?" I ask incredulously, standing in the line for food.

"I don't even remember, alright?" he rolls his eyes. "Change of topic, please?"

"Fine." I oblige. "Why are you still following me? Aren't your friends waiting for you for something?"

"Bold of you to assume I have friends." he says, and it's my turn to roll my eyes.

"I find it hard to believe that." I drawl, taking a plate and holding it out for a little mashed potatoes. I don't take anything else, but pause when Kile asks for another pudding cup but the mean old lunch lady glares and barks "One for one student!"

"One please." I say, extending my plate to her and she literally throws a cup onto mine, glaring at the next student.

"She's in a bad mood." Kile grumbles, grabbing a spoon and fork.

"She is, isn't she." I scan the area for my friends. I wave slightly when Donna catches my eye and beckons me over. "I've got to go."

"Oh." Kile blink. "Right."

I toss my hair back and pick up the pudding cup from my plate. I place it on his next to the one he already has and head to the table with my friends.

"Wait-" Kile starts, and then laughs. "Did you actually just take a cup to give it to me? Knowing full well that I wanted another?"

"For someone who's in the running for Valedictorian, you do speak such nonsense."

"Arryn-"

"I just wasn't hungry."

"Right. You know, you're a very obvious liar."

I stop and glance back at him. Hiding a smile, I lift a hand and say, "See you later, nerd."

My stomach is almost like a tank filled with rats as I stand in the boy's locker room, feeling my breaths come out heavier and heavier with every passing second.

"Dude, Arryn." Jason clamps a hand on my shoulder and I jump, turning around to look up at him. "Why haven't you changed?"

"Yeah, I'll do that." I clap him on his upper arm before turning back around. Swallowing, I grab my shorts and jersey before turning around and walking to the bathroom all the way at the end of the room.

"What are you doing?" Wallace, a lean dude and the best striker on the team, asks.

"I have to pee, so I thought I might as well change in there." I mutter weakly.

"Dude, the fuck?" Wallace laughs. "Are you shy to change in front of us?"

"Wha- don't be ridiculous." I feel my cheeks burn against my will as I take another step closer to the bathroom. "That's just stupid."

"You're blushing-"

"Leave him alone, Wall." I hear Hale, appearing from one of the rows already changed. "You're delaying him, and why would he fucking be shy now? We've all seen him naked like 50 thousand times since the beginning of the year."

I stop myself from reacting to those words, keeping my face sober and straight.

"Sorry bro." Wallace says, looking a peevish. "Didn't mean to get you late."

"It's alright man." I reassure him. "I just really gotta pee."

Glad that I was able to escape, and eternally grateful to Hale, I go inside the stall and change. But then I actually have to pee, so I pee.

Coming out, I feel relieved that the room has almost emptied out completely, and only a few remain.

"Let's go." Peter calls out, adjusting the laces of his shoes before standing up, looking at me expectantly.

"Yeah, one sec." I shove my clothes into my locker and shut it. We both exit the locker room and jog down the track and onto the field. Our locker rooms have two doors, one being an inside entrance and one that directly leads out to the field.

"Gather up, boys!" I hear coach's whistle, and can't stop the small smile at his gruff voice and familiarity he brought with him. "Donatello, good to see you."

"Good to be back, coach." I say, joining the horizontal line the rest of the guys were in.

Coach is huge, a whooping 6'6", and he was a professional player before his wife died; he quit because he needed to stay at home to take care of and raise his kids. He has brown hair, and a slight 4 'o' clock shadow, his body built with muscles and broad shoulders. He's by far one of the most popular teachers in our school, especially with the girls. He's so good looking that the school feared to keep him as they didn't want any illegal relationships. But Coach shoots down any confessions faster than the speed of light, and is the most wanted soccer teacher of all time, so the school can't let him go.

"Alright, chatting over, let's get to work." he blows his whistle loudly, and smirks at all of us, his eyed finally zeroing on me. "Donatello, for your welcome back gift, we're going to start with 15 laps of this field."

A series of groans emanate through us, and Peter and Gary on either side punch my arm.

"No lazy asses on my field!" he screams, and then blows his whistle. "On your mark, get set - what are y'all waiting for, get your asses going!"

I haven't done such strenuous exercise in over a week, and true, it doesn't seem that bad at first since it's a short period of time. But I'm pretty sure what I spent my last week doing is termed as negative exercise, and before I even finish my 3rd lap my legs are burning.

It doesn't get any better after that. Coach really pulls everything out of us today. We don't even play soccer, just exercise and exercise. And after that, what do we do?

Exercise even more.

"Holy fuck I can't feel my legs." Hale groans, lying flat on his stomach next to me on the artificial grass. I'm sitting up, tilting my head up to the sky.

"Same." I breath, still panting. "Ah come on." I force myself to stand up and look down at Hale. "I'm going before all the showers are hogged."

"Wait for me!" I hear his wail as I walk over wobbly legs to the locker room. I just want to get my legs back to how they were, because walking on unsteady legs reminds me of that day. Jesus Christ, how come even the littlest of things remind me of my worst nightmare?

Grabbing a towel and my clothes, I walk to the cubicle all the way at the end. I hang the towel and clothes on the railing attached on the outer side of the door, and step inside before locking it.

Peeling off my sweaty clothes, I fling them up and drape them over the door. After a hot shower, I slowly unlock it, still clutching the handle tightly. I'm scared to open it for some reason.

You need to get your clothes idiot. Just open it. Nobody will do anything.

I never used such speed before, but the way I opened the door and grabbed my things, people said that it looked like a shadow.

Drying myself down, I put my clothes on and step out.

"Finally! How long do you take, Ariana?" Jefferson mocks, walking in with a towel draped over his shoulder.

"Sorry sorry." I call back, walking to my locker and grabbing my stuff.

"Guys, want to chill at Blue's or something?" Gary asks, walking out of one of the cubicles in only a towel.

"I'm down." Peter says, stuffing his dirty clothes in his bag. I wrinkle my nose at that, taking my own cloth bag out to keep my clothes in it, neatly folded, before putting that bag into my backpack.

"Hale?" Gary asks, walking into our row. "Arryn?"

"Uh, yeah sure." Hale says, his eyes trained to his shoes as he took them off. "Rin, you coming?"

"Nah I can't." I shake my head, trying to sound apologetic. "Mom grounded me, remember?"

"Fuck I forgot." Gary says, removing his towel. Hale covers his cheeks with his hands, eyes closed tightly shut as he exhales loudly.

"That's too bad." he says in a voice too quiet, one that's different than his usual one.

I frown at that. Why is he acting so weird? He's been like this since morning.

When Gary leaves and goes to Wallace, I sit beside my best friend.

"What's wrong?" I ask, worried. "Are you not feeling well?"

"What? No, I'm perfectly fine." he says, blinking in surprise. "Why do you ask?"

"You've been acting weird. Since morning." I answer.

"Have I?" He laughs, but it sounds pathetic to even my ears. "Guess I'm just sleepy."

"Are you sure?" I'm still not convinced.

"Yes, I'm sure Arryn." he says, rolling his eyes.

"You'll tell me though, right? If something is wrong?" I say, and felt like such a damn hypocrite because how can I expect him to spill his secrets when I don't even tell him mine?

"Of course, dude." he clamps my shoulder. "I'll tell you if something's wrong."

"Good." I say, and stand up.

I'm still not convinced.

08-HIS room

C hapter 8

His room______________

"You're late."

I raise an eyebrow and made a big show of looking at my watch.

"By thirty seconds." I say, and Kile shrugs.

"30 seconds of my life wasted." he sticks out his tongue. "You know, you can save a life in 30 seconds. Do you understand, Arryn? Do you understand that I could have saved a life instead of waiting for you?"

"Yes yes, I understand." I deadpan, walking past him to go inside the theatre room. I pause when I saw people inside.

"What are you doing here?" One of them, a boy with freckles and glasses, asks.

Another girl, probably an 11th grader, blushes when I make eye contact with her and nudges the boy.

"It's fine, he can come here." she gushes, smiling widely. "Arryn Donatello, right?"

God, it's so obvious what she's trying to do. I don't believe even for a second that she doesn't know who I am.

"We'll just go somewhere else." Kile says. "We usually study here, but since you're already using it, it's fine."

The other 5 kids look at each other, and shrug.

"We've resumed Theatre club because exams just got over for us." One of them explains. "We'll be coming here everyday after school."

"Well shit." I sigh. "Guess we need to find another place to work, right?"

"We'll leave you to it." Kile says, and shuts the door as we leave. "Shit, this kind of puts us in a tough spot."

"What? Why?" I ask. "We can just use another room."

"no we can't, because they're all locked." Kile explains. "All rooms except the theatre room and AV room are locked, and both are being used as of today."

"Uh, library?" I suggest.

"No way, I can't eat chips there." he denies, and I roll my eyes.

"I'm sure you can hold off on eating chips for 90 minutes-"

"Don't say such blasphemous things!" Kile gasps, clutching his chest. "Why, oh why, Arryn! Why must you wound my like this?!"

"Dear God." I mutter, and then shrugged. "Guess we could go to my place. It's pretty much free. Except my little bro will bother us."

"I have a better idea." Kile says. "Let's go to my place."

"Okay. Doesn't matter either way to me."

"Cool!" he chirps, and tugs my arm to go to the front entrance. I tense at that, breathing sharply at the foreign contact that I've been trying to avoid all this time.

Thankfully he lets go when I start walking, and I follow him out of the doors.

"Should we take one car, or will you come in yours?" Kile asks, and I take one look at his car before saying, "I'll just come in mine."

Kile's eyes glint in amusement as if he knows what I thought, and I can't help the slight embarrassment that courses through me. Walking to my car, I can feel his laser sharp eyes boring into my back.

Starting up the engine, I reverse out of the parking lot, and just follow Kile's car as he heads down the road. I recognise almost everything on the way, except instead of going into Mulberry street, he takes the road to Jennifer square. Figures, he is pretty middle class.

He leads me down a road of cute, brown houses until he stops in front of one that says Dankworth Residence, 794.

Parking behind him, I get out and join him at the porch.

"This is such a cute house." I can't help saying, as I wait for him to unlock the door.

Kile snorts and looks back at me. "You're such a richie rich."

I don't refute him, trailing after him inside and closing the door.

"Wow, it's quiet." I say, lowering my voice because it feels like if I talk too loudly I would disrupt something. I am used to being greeted loudly by Mika or Mom whenever I come back home after practice.

"My parents aren't home." Kile tosses the keys into a bowl on the shoe cabinet and removes his shoes. I follow suit, placing them neatly on the rack and stepping further in. Something about the house is so...cold. Like nobody ever lives in it. It is compact and pretty nice, a normal house, but it doesn't feel like people live in it.

"Are they at work?" I ask. We go to the living room where he gestures for me to sit on the sofa.

"Yeah." he nods. "Can I get you anything? Water? Juice? A nice glass of hot chocolate?"

"Oh no thanks, I'm good." I decline. I am pretty apprehensive of taking edible and drinkable items from others. It's not like I don't trust Kile, it's just that I don't, well I don't really feel safe anywhere except for my house.

"Are you sure?" Kile asks again. "I make a mean hot chocolate."

"Yep, pretty sure."

"Alright then. Let's go up." he turns to the stairs, and I blink at him. "What?" he frowns.

"We're going up?" I ask, and he nods slowly.

"Yes. I mean, I thought we'd study in my room..." he trails off, and I swallow before nodding.

"Yeah, right. Of course." I say, standing up. "Your room is upstairs?"

"Yeah." he replies, already walking up the stairs. "We can stay down here if you-"

"No no, let's go up." I cut him off. So we will be studying in his room. Which is upstairs. It's closed off, and it is far away from the door.

Do I have my phone? I check to see quickly before reassuring myself that I am being silly and that Kile wouldn't try to assault me.

I keep the emergency number ready just incase.

"Wow, this is a nice room." I comment, looking at the walls of dark blue and white.

"Thanks." Kile says, closing the door. My eyes follow the handle and I silently register that it hasn't been locked, but it does have one.

"This bed is..." I pause and feel a small bubble of laughter rise in my throat. It's also white and blue, but there are baby sharks painted on the base.

"I've had this bed since I was 4, okay?" he protests, keeping his stuff down and peeling off his jacket. "Believe it or not, it was originally snails."

"Snails?" I echo. "Why?"

"That's what I want to know." he laughs, and jumps on his bed. "Come on, sit."

I lower myself slowly onto the mattress, keeping myself closest to the door. He has a twin bed, so it's pretty tiny. I sit against the headboard and Kile sits criss cross apple sauce in front of me.

"Okay, what were we doing last time?" he asks, taking out his note-book.

The next hour is filled with him just teaching me stuff, and me trying to distract him whenever I get bored.

"Arryn, pay attention."

"But it's boring." I half whine, lying against his pillows comfortably now, hugging one to my chest. "I can't take anymore of this."

"Fine." Kile gives up, throwing his hands in the air. "You're a lost cause."

"Hey, at least I'm not at risk of failing." I point out. "I'm pretty sure I can get a C in the next test."

"You can get an A plus if you put your mind to it." Kile purses his lips, and I groan.

"But I don't want to."

"Okay okay." he relents. "We'll stop for today."

"Yes." I agree, settling further into his soft pillows. "How do you sleep on such a tiny bed?" I ask, and can't help wrinkling my nose a bit. "I bet my feet would fall off."

"It's not tiny." Kile says dryly. "You're just used to triple king sized beds."

"I've only ever slept on triple king sized beds on vacation, for your kind information." I refute, and Kile presses his lips together, containing his laughter.

"You're so spoiled."

"I'm not spoiled." I answer, a bit appalled that he would call me that. "I just...have stuff." I finish lamely.

"You have everything." Kile says, resting his head on his palm. "Do you have anything you want or wish to have?"

Yes, my virginity.

"No, not really." I reply quietly. We're silent for a few seconds, just in each other's company before I say, "Hey Kile?"

"Hmm?"

"Can I ask you something?" I keep my eyes down at the pillow, refusing to look at him.

"Yeah, sure." I feel him shift closer, and I lean in as well, on reflex.

"Can you get something back once you've lost it?" I ask, and hold my breath as I wait for his answer. The mood has completely shifted. It feels melancholy and somber, but Kile isn't complaining, so I hope I didn't make him feel bad.

"Depends on what." I hear him say. "If it's materialistic, probably. Maybe. Probably not if you dropped it in an ocean or something."

"What about...something else?"

"Something else?" Kile stops, as if waiting for me to elaborate. When I don't, he continues by saying, "I don't know. There's a pretty great possibility though. When you've lost something, it's not as if it's wiped out of existence. It has just passed on to someone else. So yes, there's always a chance it'll find it's way back to you, or you'll find your way back to it."

Passed on? Does that mean that the innocence, the piece of me I lost that night is with that man? The man who raped me? If I know who he is, and if I confront him, does that mean I'll get it back?

Even as those thoughts run through my head, I know they are futile because I don't know who he is, nor can I ever get something like my virginity back. It's unheard of, and out of the realm of possibility.

Once you lose it, you can't get it back.

I smile and look at Kile.

"I should get going now." I say, pushing myself up. Kile looks surprised and he scrambles off the bed.

"Why? You can stay for some more time. I don't mind." he tells me, but I shake my head.

"I should get going. Mika and Mum will start worrying. And I'm grounded." I laugh half-heartedly, walking to the door after grabbing my things.

"Okay, I'll see you tomorrow?" he asks as we walk down the stairs.

"Yeah, I'll see you tomorrow." I say. I look back at Kile, his half messy hair, pink cheeks and the brightest eyes I've ever seen. Even though what he said doesn't hold true for me, it does make me feel better. And I'm thankful for that.

09-CAUGHT

C hapter 9

Caught_______________

"I'm here to see Dr. George. He asked me to come in today?" I peer down at the familiar secretary, leaning over the counter.

"Oh right. Arryn Donatello, right?" she asks, and I nod. "Great, go on up. He should be free now."

"Thank you." I say, turning around and heading for the elevators. I had to skip practice for this, making up some excuse about my mother wanting me home. I know that this visit is important, and can't help but feel that Dr. George was lying when he said it's only to pick up some forms.

I ride to floor 2 and make my way to room 17. I look inside and softly knock on the door when I see him sitting all alone inside.

Dr. George looks up and his face brightens. He gestures for me to come inside, standing up.

"Good evening." I greet, stepping in.

"Evening evening." he smiles. "Arryn, have a seat. I'll be right with you."

"Alright." I sit down on the chair and wait for him to get some papers from his cabinet.

"You came directly from school?" he asks.

"Yeah." I confirm. "So, where are the forms?"

He sighs, and says, "Arryn, you seem like a smart boy. I'm sure you figured out that I called you for a reason other than picking up your forms."

The nagging fear I had the whole day doubles. "Do I have some disease?"

"No no." he denies quickly. "You're completely clean. By the way," he picks up one of the sheets of paper he got and shows it to me. "You're HIV test is negative. You're completely clean, Arryn."

"Oh thank god." I slack back in my chair, sending a silent prayer to the heavens. "Wait, so why did you call me?"

"Arryn, I'm a doctor." he says, looking serious. "I've been a doctor for almost 20 years now. And I can make out the difference between sex and...non-consensual sex. We have standard procedure for that."

"What." I blink at him, not comprehending what he's saying.

"I-" he stops and takes a deep breath, as if preparing himself. "Arryn, that night you had unprotected sex, are you sure you both were drunk?"

"What are you saying." My voice is tight, barely squeezing through my throat as I clutch the HIV test results in my hands.

"I'm saying," he pauses and leans forward, "Arryn, I think you're not telling me everything that happened that night. You were raped, weren't you?"

I don't know what's happening anymore. My vision is blurry, I can't feel myself, I can't feel anything around me and there's a sharp, high ringing in my ears. My face is hot and the beats of my heart burst in my ears like thunder and before I even know what I'm doing, I'm standing up.

"Arryn, please sit down-"

"No." I try to sling my arm through the arm of my bag but I keep missing and I grit my teeth in frustration. "No."

"Arryn-"

"You don't know what you're talking about." Frantic. "We were both drunk. I wasn't..." Frightened.

"Arryn what happened that night wasn't sex-"

"Stop saying that!" I scream, squatting down and covering my ears. "Stop saying that! Stop saying sex! I hate it! I hate it I hate it I hate it! Stop saying it!"

"Okay okay." Dr. George says, rounding the table. He stops a few feet in front of me and also squats down, eye level with me. "Arryn, I'm sorry."

"No." I whisper. "No. I wasn't raped."

I hear him exhale softly, and the tears jump in my eyes.

"I wasn't." I breathe, refusing to let the tears fall down. "I wasn't."

"Arryn." Dr. George whispers. "Arryn, you're just a child. It's okay. It's okay to be scared. It's okay to admit it."

"No." I insist, and stand up abruptly. "I have to go."

"Please, wait for a moment-"

"Thank you for your concern, Dr. George. But I have to go." I exhale, before hurrying out of the room. I hear him step out and can feel him looking at me as I run away.

I take the elevator down and bolt out of the lobby. The secretary flashes me a concerned look when she sees me pass by, almost standing up but I give her a wobbly smile to reassure her before stepping out.

I keep taking deep breaths to hold off the sobs as I walk to the car. Sliding in behind the wheel, I toss my bag on the passenger seat before exiting the hospital parking lot.

I don't know where exactly I drive, but I drive for almost 45 minutes before stopping next to a deserted park as it starts drizzling. I don't recognise the place I'm in, but I don't care as I press my forehead to the wheel.

As the rain patters around me, all I can do is scream and sob and hit the wheel again and again. I'm angry and scared and I don't think there's any hope left in me.

It isn't fair. It isn't fair. Why me? What have I ever done? Is it because I'm a spoiled rich brat who has everything in life easy? Is it because I take everything for granted? Is it because, is it because, is it because...?

I wrap my arms around myself and squeeze my eyes shut, before opening them immediately when flashbacks attack me.

He hit me when I tried to fight back, spreading my knees open so that I couldn't hide from him, so that I was completely vulnerable and he took advantage of it. He took advantage of me.

His hands were so big, they had no problem holding me down. I hated how the course skin felt on mine. I hated how his sweaty, fat body pressed over me and crushed me down on the bed. I hated it. I hated him.

He tried to get me aroused, tried to get me hard by touching me, but no amount of fondling from him made me so. It was disgusting. Gross. I wanted to puke. But my body was sluggish and I could barely move my hands and legs. But I could feel every damn thing.

I jerk in agony and pull my hair roughly, hoping the pain will distract me from the torturous nightmare.

My lips tremble and I lean against the cold window, pretending that the streaks of water rolling down the glass pane are just leaked through rain drops.

"I would like to exit my life now." Hale groans, and I tiredly looked at him.

"I agree." I say, my head on the cool desk. "Having these many assignments should be illegal."

"It's so useless." he whines, and also leans down on his table, turning his head to look at me. "I hate school."

"Me too."

We both look up to see Donna looking down at us, pulling up a chair. "You know what I want to do?"

"Eat a burger." Hale says.

"Yes, but I also want to go skydiving." she declares. "And I want to fuck Alex Rider."

"Alex Rider?" Hale echoes. "The kids series Alex Rider?"

"Yes." she nods. "I imagine him totally hot in my head. Also, Percy Jackson."

"Oh, I imagine him totally hot in my head too." Hale grins. "Also, I'm thinking we skip the rest of the day and get burgers."

"I'm down." Donna says. They began talking about something, and I tune out as a wave of fatigue hits me and I want nothing more than just to go home and curl up on my bed.

"...Rin? Rin!"

"I'm awake!" I snap, blinking open my eyes and looking at their surprised faces. "Uh, what?"

"Dude, are you okay?" Donna asks. "You look dead."

"I'm a senior in high school. It would be weird if I didn't." I reply dryly, trying to play it off.

"You look like you haven't slept for a week." Hale says, sounding concerned. "Yesterday was Sunday. Don't tell me you didn't sleep in."

"Of course I slept in." I lie. I barely slept 3 hours. "I'm just tired is all." The previous week has consisted of me wallowing in self pity and having the basic consistency of a zombie.

"If you say so." Donna says uncertainly. "So, you down?"

"Hmm? For what?"

"For skipping."

"Uh, no. I can't." I sigh. "My mum will kill me if she finds out." It isn't a complete lie, because she would kill me. But I'm also denying because I don't think I could go through hours of walking around, shopping and pretending to be happy.

"Since when did you care about that?" Hale asks incredulously.

"Since she grounded my ass for a month."

"Ouch. Right, forgot." Hale winces, and Donna laughs.

"Come, let's go. I'm sure Jason and some other guys would like to join too. Evie has biology, so that's a no from her side." she stands up and Hale follows suit.

"Bye man." he claps my shoulder, and I wave a goodbye before slumping in my seat as they left.

I wait till the class is empty before heading to the cafeteria for lunch.

I spot Evie in line, her phone on her hand.

"Hey Evie." I say, cutting the line and joining her. A few pass dirty looks but nobody says anything.

"Hey." she smiles, putting her phone down. "I was just about to text you. Where's Hale?"

"Don and him are skipping." I grab a tray and pass her one.

"Ugh I wanna too." she mumbles. "But I-"

"- have biology." I complete for her. "They knew, that's why they didn't call."

"How come you didn't go?"

"Mum has already grounded me for a month. Can't afford anything else on my back." I shrug, and she shakes her head.

"Is that all you're taking?" she asks, looking down at my singular packet of juice and salad. "Wow, you're eating like a certified mean girl."

"You do realise you're a mean girl." I snort, walking with her to our table. "I mean, you couldn't be a meaner girl if you tried."

"Hey, I-" she stops and laughed. "I don't have a counter argument, but I do love me a four cheese margarita pizza."

"You can eat a whole, 12 inch one by yourself." I remember. "How exactly are you thin, dude?"

"It's something called exercise." she provides. We slide into our seats at our empty table. Looks like everyone else are also skipping. "And I like binge eat only on certain occasions. Not all the time."

"You know what, salad isn't even bad." I say, munching on a piece of lettuce.

"Yeah, but like," she shakes her plate of pasta. "Pasta."

I roll my eyes.

We chat all through lunch, exchanging stupid banter and teasing each other. Being with Evie is easy. After all, we've known each other for almost 14 years now. Hale, her and I all met at this get together our parents had years back. We've been best friends ever since.

"...so now every time the lights go out, Laurent yells 'Grab the salt!' all because of some stupid tv show."

"Well you could always be haunted by a ghost." I point out. "Then he'll be the one saving your ass."

"You're seriously siding with him?!" she exclaims. "But like, the actors in the show are super cute. Oh, and then there's this angel..."

I walk her to her class, stopping in front of the door.

"Fuck, my eyes are so heavy." she groans, blinking rapidly. "I'll see you after bio? Wait, you have practice right?"

"Yep." I say. "I'll call you tonight."

"I think Hale's coming over tonight." she says. "Come if you can. Ask your mum."

"Will do." I say, even though I know what my answer is.

She walks inside and I leave, heading up to math class.

Going to my usual seat, I slip in and get out my text books.

"Italian or Mexican?"

I turn my head to see who spoke to me, and relaxed when I see that it's just Kile.

"Italian." I reply, going about my stuff again.

"Really?!" he gasps. "I can't choose!"

"What is it with you and food." I ask, leaning on my forearms as he sits down beside me.

"I love it." he says seriously. "I love it. I would die for it. I would marry it if I could."

"I-"

"Arryn, Kile, please stop talking." We're interrupted my Mrs. Marionette, who's looking at us sternly. "I'm trying to teach here."

"Sorry." We both say in sync, and grin at each other.

"You both will be the death of me. I expected this from Arryn, but Kile..." she shakes her head and turns to her table. "Open to page 983. And no more talking!"

I open my text book and survey over the questions.

Ah, these are too difficult. I think, and feel my mind already wandering.

Something hits my head, and I frown as a small piece of paper falls down on my desk. Picking it up, I unfold it and read the contents it holds.

Pay attention dumbass.

My mouth opens slightly in mock shock, and I tear out a piece of paper from my own notebook, writing I am, dickwad.

I throw it at him and he bits his lip to hide his grin when it hits his cheek. He unravels it and his eyebrows raise to his hairline.

The message I get back: To think you would use such language.

I'm going to reply but suddenly realise that the entire class is silent. A peek shows the everyone looking at me, and I hold in a wince as I look up at Ms. Marionette's glaring face.

"Arryn Donatello." she says, sounding dangerous. "Kile Dankworth. What is wrong with the two of you."

I swallow and look at Kile, to find that he has also turned to look at me.

"Uh-" I start. "We, uh, he was helping me."

"Really?" she drawls. "Sora, read out the chits."

Sora, a tall lanky boy with blonde, curly hair and slight acne, swallows and looks at me helplessly. I sigh and hand him the chits. Kile copies.

"Um," he squeaks, opening the paper. "Pay attention, asshole." he recites, cheeks red.

"Next."

"To think you would use such language."

"Next."

"I am, dic-" he stops and his whole neck flushes in embarrassment. Kile's pink too, but I don't really care. I've been in way worse trouble than this.

"So, how exactly is this helping you?" she barks.

"He was telling me to pay attention." I say meekly.

"Goodness gracious me." she sounds frustrated. "Kile, Ashley, switch seats please."

I looked at Ashley, who sits in front of me. She stops running her fingers through her bob and looks back at me with barely concealed excitement.

"Okay!" she squeals, almost flying out of her seat. Kile looks extreme-ly unhappy about it, and I purse my lips, also upset.

He gets up, morosely taking his stuff and dumping them on the desk. Even though it's only in front of me, it feels far away and suddenly getting through math seems even more of an arduous task.

"Hey Arryn!" Ashley says, her voice high and irritating. "I'm so happy that we can sit together."

"Yeah." I reply, and feel my eyes shutting involuntarily. I let them close and fold my arms under my head to sleep. I hear her say something along the lines of "Oh, you seem tired..." before I slip away.

It's the loud bell signaling the end of class that wakes me up. I feel a bit bad for sleeping the whole time, but Ms. Marionette doesn't seem very angry.

"You slept the whole time." Kile accuses, and I rub my eye as I push myself up. He takes the opportunity to lean back and rest his head on my table. I look down at him upside down, and he grins as his hair flops back from his forehead. His glasses rides up and I huff a laugh before removing them and keeping them to the side.

"My head hurts." he complains.

"So does mine." I agree, and bring my fingers up to play with his hair. "Your hair's so soft."

"Of course it is." Kile says, eyes closing when I slowly massage his head. "I condition it every 3 days."

"Evie makes me use conditioner too." I say, enjoying the way his soft tresses rub against my skin. "She says only using shampoo makes it rough."

"Damn right it does." we both look up to see Evie standing there.

"When did you come in?" I ask, as she pulls up a chair and sits down.

"Just now. You both seem tired." she says, and exhales. "I'm beat. I want to go home and take a nice, hot bath."

"Same." Kile says. Evie turns to him, blinking slowly as if she's trying to figure out something.

"Who are you?" she finally says, and Kile scoffs. I hide my smile because she's always like this, she hardly remembers anybody.

"Kile." he says, and when she still remains blank, "Kile Dankworth?"

"Uh yeah." she says, in a monotone voice. "Kile Dankworth."

"You have no idea who I am, do you?" he snorts. "We met in the bathroom? When Arryn was puking?"

"Oh right." she says. "You're that... person."

"Accurate description." I laugh softly and move my fingers to the area above his ears. "Oh fuck, that feels good." he moans.

"What am I watching right now?" Evie deadpans. "Arryn's massages feel good right?"

"So good." Kile breaths. "Arryn, you have magic fingers."

"So I've been told." I reply, amused.

"Hey, aren't you that kid that banged Donna last year?" Evie suddenly says. I pause and look down at him.

"Yeah, I remember her telling me that." I say, the conversation coming back to mind. "She took your virginity!"

Kile flushes and covers his face with his hands.

"Oh my gosh, this is so embarrassing." he whines, and I laugh before prying his hands off his face.

"So?" Evie asks, and Kile looks at her in confusion. "Was it good?"

"Oh my fucking God-"

"Answer the question!" I urge, really really wanting to know for some reason.

"I don't believe you two." he murmurs, slumping down in defeat.

"Tell tell tell tell tell tell tell tell." Evie chants.

"Yes okay!" he exclaims, face red. "It was good."

"Good, really good or amazing?" I ask, and his mouth drops in incredulity.

"It was Donna Lockwood. What do you think?" he says dryly, and Evie laughs loudly.

"Amazing." We both say at the same time.

"Can you please start massaging again?" Kile pouts. I roll my eyes but press my fingers back to his head.

10-aBSenT

C hapter 10

Absent ____________

I feel his chin on my shoulder and I sigh as he puts his entire weight on me.

"Kile, get your fat ass off me." I groan, leaning on the desk as he keeps nagging me.

"But you're not listening to me!" he whines. "I'm putting my heart and soul into telling you about-"

"- how your pee was satisfactory." I deadpan. "I get it. You had a nice pee."

"But you don't get it!" he stands up and places his hands on my shoulders. "It was so so so satisfactory! It felt so liberating."

"Yes yes, good for you." I roll my eyes, leaning back and resting my head on his stomach. "Why is it so cloudy outside?" I ask as I turn my head to look out his bedroom window.

"I like cloudy. Especially in the evenings. It's so peaceful."

"Same." I agree. "I also like the smell after it rains."

"Oh god yes." he agrees, and his hands softly press down on my shoulders. "I love jumping in the puddles. And driving my car through them so that some poor person gets hit with dirty water."

"You're evil!" I laugh. "And can you fucking grade my test already? You do realise we're here to study?"

"Yeah yeah." he pulls up another chair to join me at the desk. "I'm glad we were able to finish almost 10 chapters in 3 weeks." he takes my sheet and picks up a pen.

"3 weeks? It feels so much longer than that." I tease.

"Shut up." he snorts, and gives my first answer a big, green tick. "You're not even bad at math. You're just-"

"- lazy." I finish. "You've probably told me this like 20 times by now."

"Well it's true!" he exclaims. "Good job, by the way. All the answers are right."

"For real?" I grin and take my answer sheet. "Thank fuck."

"Can we stop now?" he moans, and I roll my eyes.

"You're supposed to be the teacher, you know." I chide, but gets up and sits on his bed. "Can you switch off the fan, by the way? It's cold."

"It is, isn't it?" he switches it off and falls onto the bed with a big oomph, sending me flying up.

"Hey!" I protest, hot at being thrown so easily.

He bites his bottom lip and smiles cheekily, before his face sobers up and he rolls onto his back. I fall back against the pillows and raise an eyebrow at him.

"What is it? Spit it out." I say, and he tips his head to one side. His black hair falls over his face slightly, covering his blue eyes for a second.

"Arryn? Do you-" he pauses, and turns away, not meeting my eye. "We're friends right?"

I'm taken aback, not expecting that.

"What do you mean?" I ask, and he rolls back onto his stomach, peering up at me through his lashes.

"Like, you're Arryn Donatello. The Arryn Donatello. Girls want to be with you, guys want to be you-"

"Kile."

"I'm just saying," he sounds frustrated, "why would you want to spend time with me, when you already have so many friends?"

I stay silent, quietly comprehending his question.

Why am I hanging out with Kile?

Is it because of an obligation I feel with him being my teacher? Or is it because I feel sorry for him? Is it because I just need to be with someone who doesn't know me?

No.

I smile and pat his head.

"Idiot. I'm obviously your friend." I say softly.

"But why?" he asks.

"Do I need a reason?" I top my head. "I'm your friend because I like you, obviously."

He blinks in surprise, and then starts laughing.

"What?" I exclaim, blushing. "Why are you laughing?"

"Because- because you-" he breaks out into another fit of laughter, rolling onto his back yet again and clutching his stomach. "You literally over simplified the whole concept of friendship."

"Well yeah." I blubber. "Why else would I be your friend? I can hardly imagine someone being friends with someone who they don't like."

"Isn't it deeper than that?" Kile muses. "At least the books and movies say that."

"Friendship isn't complicated." I say, going back to patting his head. "If you like someone, be their friend."

"What if you stop liking them?"

"Then try to understand why you dislike them." I shrug. "If you like someone, it's obviously because of some characteristic or traits, right? And nobody's perfect. Your friend might become sad, or angry, or depressed. It's when they make you dislike them that they need you to be their friend the most."

Kile is silent, and the only thing heard in the room is the soft sound of our breathing synchronizing.

"Arryn?"

"Hmm?"

"I'm glad we're friends."

"Why am I here?"

I groan softly when Hale tuggs me forward into the empty classroom. He grins at me and closes the door once we're inside.

"So, we're here to..." he pauses for dramatic effect, "plan Evie's surprise birthday party!!"

"Oh." I say. It isn't that I'm not excited, but I already know that Hale will end up planning the whole damn thing himself, because he just loves, well, planning things.

"It's the big one eight!" he squeals, turning around and gesturing for Donna, who is already inside and sitting on a desk, to join us. "We need to throw a really, really, big party for her!"

"Okay, so what are we doing?" I ask, sitting down on a chair. Hale makes an excited noise and removes some sheets from his bag. Donna and I sigh simultaneously, and then exchange small smiles. She reaches out and ruffles my hair, sitting on the desk next to my head.

I'm slowly getting used to the touching again. It makes me a bit uncomfortable when people I don't know try to be too friendly with me, but when it's just my friends I'm okay. I don't know why, but I think my body is able to recognise their touches now, and I'm able to rein in my responses pretty well. I'm surprised at how close I've gotten to Kile as well. After all, it's been just a little over 3 weeks. I guess friendship does build fast.

Where is he, anyway? I think, leaning on my palms. I haven't seen him since morning. Is he absent?

"Rin, you're spacing out!" Hale's voice snaps through me, and I apologetically look at him as I straighten myself out and force myself to stop thinking about that boy.

"Yes yes, continue." I urge, and he goes back to excitedly talking about the party.

After skipping 2 classes and Hale chewing our ears off, we settle on... I don't even know. Hale decides something he is happy with and Don and I just go with it.

"Hey, have you seen Kile today?" I ask, as we leave the classroom.

"Who?" Hale asks.

"That guy you keep hanging with?" Donna says, applying some lip balm on her mouth.

"Yeah. I haven't seen him since morning." I say. "Is he absent or something?"

"I don't know. I haven't seen him today." Donna muses. She is a science student, like him, so they share classes. "Hale?"

"I haven't either." Hale says. "Wait, who are we talking about?"

"No, it's fine." I wave him off, and purse my lips.

Is he absent? That's odd, because he is the most straight laced student I know. Is he sick? He always waits for me in the morning, or at least comes and says hi. Wait, is he mad because he always has to wait for me? Oh god, what if he is really sick and collapsed or something?

"Hey guys, I'll be right back." I say, taking out my phone and dialing his number.

The call goes through, but doesn't connect. I ring again, but he still doesn't pick up.

Inconvenient fire drill

Me : [Hey, are you absent?]

Sent.

I wait for a reply, but none comes. I push down the concern I'm feeling and go back to Hale and Donna.

"Did he answer?" Hale asks, and I shake my head. "Maybe he's sick. And sleeping."

"Maybe." I agree quietly.

"Well, let's go to lunch. I'm hungry as fuck." Donna says, linking her arms through mine and Hale's to drag us in the direction of the cafeteria. A boy passing us turns red when he sees Donna, and she smirks before winking at him.

"Don't tell me you-" Hale brakes off and Donna devilishly smirks again.

"I don't know what you're talking about. "She replies with fake innocence.

"Hey guys." Evie smiles, joining us as we walk down the cafeteria to the food line. "Hello, my significant bother." she greets Hale.

"Hello to you too, my cherished inevitable downfall." Hale replies sticking out his tongue.

"TV static."

"Wet sock."

"Pee stain."

"Wailing baby." Hale pauses. "On an airplane!"

"Okay!" Donna exclaims, stopping them. "That's enough, kiddos. Get your plates and eat your food."

Hale and Evie roll their eyes at the same time, but dutifully grab their plates and take their food.

"I'm not hungry." I decline the tray Evie holds out to me.

"What's up with you? Are you okay?" Evie asks, as we all sit down at our table.

"He's all bunched up because Kile didn't show up at school today." Donna explains.

Evie looks at me and raises an eyebrow. "He's absent."

"Yeah." I say. "And he's not picking up my calls. Or responding to my texts."

"Oh I see." she says, and gets this look in her eyes. "Maybe he's sick. And sleeping."

"That's what I said!" Hale cries through a mouthful of beans.

I tune out of the conversation, my mind wandering to where Kile is and if he is in trouble. It is almost excruciating going through the rest of school before I run out of there.

"Dude, what about practice?" Hale asked, stopping me in the hallway.

"Tell coach that I have a family emergency." I said. Hale looked unhappy, so I gave him the best pleading eyes I could and he caved.

"Fine! But remember that you owe me!" he hollered as I bustled down the corridor.

I first drive to a supermarket to get some stuff like vitamin juice, ginger drinks and cup soup. I don't know how to cook, so I grab a can of ready made sauce just in case. He must have pasta in his house, right? It takes me a while to find everything because I've never been to a super market before, and I keep having to exchange things because they have dirt on it.

Billing everything out, I make my way to his house and ring the door bell. I wait for a few minutes, worrying my lower lip as the only thing that greets me was dead silence.

I ring the bell again.

It feels almost forever before I hear faint footsteps and the door pops open, only a crack.

"Kile?" I ask hesitantly, trying to get a look inside.

"Arryn?" His voice is hoarse and thick, as if he's been crying. I would know, I've cried my voice even hoarser and thicker than this.

"Hey dude. Are you okay?" I ask, relieved when he finally opens the door completely.

"Yeah, I'm fine." he says, swallowing and not looking at me. But I can still see the redness in his sclera and the way he sniffs subtly.

"Kile, what's wrong?" I ask, walking forward and kind of forcing my way inside. "You look really bad."

"I-" he sounds so defeated, so sad, that I couldn't take it anymore. I know he doesn't want to talk about it. Nobody wanted to talk about it, especially when the wound is still this fresh.

"I'm going to make some pasta." I say, walking in determinedly after shutting the door.

"What?" he sounds incredulous. I say nothing more as I grab his elbow and steer him to the sofa, pushing him gently onto it.

"Here, drink this." I order, giving him a vitamin juice, peach flavoured. "It tastes like iced tea."

"You don't have to-"

"Shush." I say, switching on the tv and flipping onto a comedy channel. "Watch this." I instruct.

Kile blinks at me, and he looks like he wants to argue but ends up giving in and slumping into the sofa. He opens the cap of the bottle and takes a gulp.

"This is yummy." he whispers. I smile and go to his kitchen.

Okay, time to start cooking and hope the fantastic culinary skills of my mom somehow passes onto me.

First, get a bowl to boil pasta.

It feels weird rummaging around in someone else's kitchen, but I finally find a bowl like thingie that seems big enough, so I put it on the stove before pouring in water. While it heatsd up a little, I search for pasta, which is thankfully stored in a drawer. Adding a bit of salt and oil to the water (I read that online), I add the penne pasta and wait for it to cook.

I heat up the soup I bought in the mean time. Thankfully, the only thing I need to do with the pasta sauce is heat it in a pan.

It takes me about 15 minutes to get everything ready, and I carefully carry the bowl of soup in one hand and the plate of pasta in the other to Kile in the sofa.

"Oh wow, I didn't know you could cook." he says, voice softer than usual as I join him on the sofa. He is watching some sitcom about three families all related to each other.

"I can't." I say. "This is ready made sauce pasta, and cup soup."

"Cup soup?" Kile huffs a laugh and I feels a little warmth at that. It is nice seeing him with a smile, even if it is half forced. Kile is always happy. He is never sad. I don't like sad Kile.

He takes a sip of the soup, blowing on the spoon a bit before putting it in his mouth. "It's good." he says. "It's really good."

I feel embarrassed by that and shove the plate of pasta to him. "Here, eat this."

Kile looks at the bowl in his hands, and then back at me. I furrow my brows, and he raises one of his. I catch on to his insinuation and my jaw falls apart.

"I'm not feeding you." I deny obstinately.

I am rebutted with a loud, pitifully clogged sniff.

"Fine." I grumble, stabbing a piece of pasta with the fork. "I don't believe you're making me feed you." I grumble again, holding out the fork to him.

He grins cheekily before leaning forward and wrapping his pink lips around the spokes. Leaning back, he chews it slowly and gives me a thumbs up.

"It's tasty." he confirms, and I snort.

"I didn't even make it." I shake my head, giving him another piece. I just then notice that he isn't wearing his glasses right now. I can see his eyes clearly, and the way his thick eyelashes softly touch his cheek every time he blinks. "You have pretty eyes." I point it, and he turns to look at me. His cheeks are flushed the lightest pink, and his lips are slightly parted. I don't know if it is because he was crying or something, but all his features are so prominent, right then.

"Yours are prettier." he says, voice rough and deeper than I've ever heard before. We look at each other silently, before I take some more pasta on the fork and hold it out to him.

"Open up, Dankworth." I say, and he closes his eyes before opening his mouth.

"Will you come to school tomorrow?" I ask, and Kile doesn't answer immediately.

"Do you want me to?"

"Well, you usually say hi to me in the morning. And tomorrow's Thursday, which means we have tuition. And, by the way, you don't have to wait for me in the morning, you know? I don't expect you to. I guess I'm kind of used to it, though. But it's fine. I'll wait instead. I'll stand on top of the steps and wait for you if you want. After all, if you miss school it'll be bad on your college apps. So yeah. I'll wait. For you." I finish my awkward speech and press my lips together to physically prevent myself from blabbering even more.

Kile's lips tug upwards as he smiles, actually smiles for the first time today and puts his hand over his eyes.

"You-" he exhales and took another sip of his soup. "I'll be there tomorrow."

"Good." I huff, trying to play it off as if it doesn't matter to me. "Great. Good. Cool."

"Yes, cool." he repeats, sounding amused. "Now, give me another damn pasta, Rin."

11-misunderstandings

C hapter 11

Misunderstanding_______________________________

"You know what, I'm so done with life."

I glance at Hale, who is slumped against the lockers. "I hate every-thing." he grumbles, sliding down until he's squatting. "You know what I want right now?"

"Pizza?" I guess, and he groans again.

"Fuck me. Fuck you. Fuck the world. I want to cry." I reach my hand down to pull him up. He grasps it and gets up.

"Why don't we go for pizza this weekend?" I ask.

"For real? But your mum-"

"My grounding ends this Friday." I smirk, leaning against the lockers. "One month, baby."

"Fuck yeah!" he exclaims, throwing his hands up in the air and crashing into me. "You're coming over, we're chilling in my heated jacuzzi with pizza and beer."

"Right." I say. I will not be drinking. Or removing my clothes. I'll just have to talk my way out of it.

"Hey guys." Gary comes up to us, pausing to bro hug.

"Hey." I greet.

"Hey." Hale also says, voice unusually high. "Hey Gary."

"So, get this, coach cancelled training today." he says.

"Why?" I ask. I'm just getting my mojo back, and coach is cancelling?

"One of his kids is sick." he sighs. "He needs to go and visit at the hospital after school."

"Oh shit." I say. Hale's brows furrow.

"Crap, that sucks. Will the kid be okay, though?"

"Yeah pretty much. Just a mild case of the flu." Gary nods. "But she's pretty young, so the hospital wanted to keep her over night just incase. He needs to pick her up today."

"Is there practice tomorrow?" I ask, because I have tuition tomorrow and won't have time.

"Nah, I don't think he's keeping it tomorrow. Probably early morning one day." he shrugs, and I nod.

"Cool." Gary and Hale go to their classes, and I'm going to go as well when my phone buzzes.

Inconvenient fire drill

Kile : [You free rn]

Me : [I have something called class]

Kile : [Up for cutting?]

Me : [Are you serious? Is Kile, the valedictorian, the smartest, goodiest two shoes, teacher's pet and irritating wet sock actually asking to skip class?]

Kile : [Bitch I'm not valedictorian yet]

Me : [Yet. Your arrogance never fails to amaze me]

Kile : [Please? I'm at the bleachers. I'm bored af. I'm so ahead they literally can't teach me anything new]

Me : [Fine, but you better take responsibility if I fail]

Kile : [Aren't you already?]

Me : [Couldn't hear you over the sound of my middle finger getting a boner :)]

I pocket my phone and push my books back into the locker. Won't be needing those.

Turning around, I go down the corridor and pass the classrooms, heading to the back door. Walking out, I make my way to the field, scanning the seats for a familiar face.

I spot him a second later, his dark, unruly hair sticking out in all directions as he sits on one of the higher seats. It's cold and windy, so I pull my hoodie sleeves over my fingers to get warmer.

"What's up." I greet, walking down the aisle and sliding into the cold, metal seat next to his.

"Hey." he grins sloppily, and I immediately get suspicious.

"Okay, what did you do?" I ask, narrowing my eyes.

"What makes you think I did anything?" he scoffs, trying to sound offended but it doesn't faze me.

"Because you just gave me your Oh, I made a slight mess but it's not actually slight but a very big mess smile." I huff, and he scoffs again.

"To think you would push such accusations on me without eligible proof- Okay so I tore my pants." he grumbles. I stare at him silently for a few moments, willing him to say Just kidding!

"What?" is my intelligent answer.

"I-" he exhales and stands up, before turning around slowly and showing me his behind.

A laugh chokes my throat, and I clamp a hand over my mouth to stop the fits of giggles threatening to escape. When he gestures to the piece of cloth stuck to the handle of the chair, I lose it and burst out laughing.

"W-wha- What the fuck!" I holler, slapping my thigh as he stands there with pouty lips and a scowl. "Y-you, did you freaking tear open your pants o-on the chair-"

"I get it I get it!" he cries. "It's funny! But I still need damage control and for you to somehow get me a new pair of pants."

"I-I-" I break out into another round of laughter, making him turn again to look at the bright blue underwear he is wearing under nor-mal tracks.

"Who even wears track pants to school?" I ask, once I've finally calmed down. "You were basically asking for it."

"And that's the cruel mindset of this world." Kile exclaims. "Blaming the victim! Grow up, Arryn. We live in a modern, forward looking society."

"Okay okay, I'll get you pants." I say, rolling my eyes.

"You just have an extra pair?" he asks, surprised.

"Yeah." I yawn. I always carry extra clothes with me these days. Just... incase. "Wait here."

I rush back inside and to my locker, taking out my bag and searching for the pair of pants. It's normal yoga pants, one that I wouldn't ever wear in public unless forced, but Kile seems okay with it so.

I go back and smile when I see him sitting in the same spot, looking down at his phone.

"Here." I say, handing him the pair and sitting down with a huff. "I just ran for you, so you better be eternally grateful to me."

"Sir yes sir." he says, taking the pants with a grateful smile. "You're the best, Arryn."

I feel a bit embarrassed by that, and look away as I feel a light heat coat my cheeks.

"Fuck it's freezing." I turn around to see him hopping from one leg to another as he stands in only his underwear.

"Kile!" I exclaim, humiliated beyond expression as I cover my eyes with my palms. I can still see a bit through the cracks between my fingers. "Don't strip here!"

"It's fine, no one's here." he dismisses, sliding on my tracks. "Ah they're slightly loose."

"What?" I ask, lowering my hands.

"You have wider hips than me." he smirks, and my face flames as I scramble for words.

"I- don't have wider hips than you!" I stutter. "Idiot!"

He laughs and sits down next to me with a long, drawn out exhale.

"Your pants are so comfortable." he mumbles. "They're really warm."

"That's just gay man." I laugh, and Kile looks at me, not laughing.

"Is that a bad thing?" he asks quietly, and I snort.

"Obviously. It's disgusting." I say.

"Being gay is disgusting?" he repeats, and I nod.

"Yep. Unnatural."

"I wish you wouldn't say that." he snaps, suddenly sounding very angry and serious. "It's not very nice."

"It's the truth though." I shrug. "Why does it matter to you anyway?"

"Why?" he lets out a laugh, but it isn't like his other laughs that are light and happy and warm. "Because you're being homophobic."

"But it isn't right." I stress. "Why does it even matter to you? It's not like your gay." I snicker. Kile remains quiet, and in that moment, I feel a slight tension stretch between us.

"You're not, right?" I ask, trying to appear cool but inside I'm struggling to maintain my emotions. "You're not gay. You slept with Don."

"I'm not." he whispers. I relax, until he continues, "I'm bisexual."

I don't hear him correctly.

"What?" I ask, voice tight and strained as I look at him. "What are you saying, Kile? If this is a joke, it isn't funny." The air around me becomes sharper, and I can feel the tips of my ears going hot as he maintains terribly heated eye contact with me.

"I'm not joking." he says. "I've never tried to hide it. It just hasn't come up before. I'm bi."

"No you're not." I hiss, and his eyes turn cold. "Take that back, Kile. You're not bisexual."

"What is wrong with you?" he sounds frustrated, shocked. "Why are you being such a jackass? It's not like I came out as a terrorist."

"Well that would be better than you wanting to fuck guys!" It comes out before I can even process what I'm saying. The way his face falls is almost in slow motion. I can make out the light leaving his eyes, his cheeks turning red, his mouth parting in disbelief and the sheer shock reflecting on his entire body.

"What the hell?!" he screams, standing up as he looks down at me in fury. "Are you insane? Did you just say that being gay is worse than being a terrorist?!"

I don't reply. I'm scared. He is towering over me and I'm so fucking scared. I don't like it when he yells.

"I thought-" he breaks off and runs a hand through his hair. "Why? Me liking guys isn't hurting you in anyway! Why does it matter?!"

Please don't yell.

When I don't answer, his eyes fill with tears and he furiously wipes them away.

"I thought you were a decent person." he spits, gathering his things. "I never pegged you for a fucking homophobic bitch."

"It's wrong." I whisper, sinking into my seat when he whips around to glare at me. "Kile, it's okay. We can still fix it-"

"It's not something than can be fixed!" he advances towards me and I try to move away but he is taking up all the space and I can't find an exit.

"Plea-"

"I thought we were becoming close." he chuckles dryly, clutching his fists. "I thought- we-"

"You're just confused-"

"Shut up." he growls, so menacing that my hands start trembling and my eyes start watering. Please. Stop it. Don't get mad.

"You're a fucking bastard." he pauses, eyes flashing with anger I didn't know Kile, my Kile, my friendly Kile, such a ray of sunshine, could ever hold. "You're disgusting."

Something snaps, and I can't feel anything anymore as he turns heel and walks away. My hands won't stop shaking, my entire body is numb.

Disgusting.

He's right. You are disgusting. You're a fucking whore. You slept with some man who you don't even remember. You're dirty. You're so fucking dirty.

I bury my head in my hands. I can't feel anything.

I don't even know if I'm crying.

I go home. I couldn't bare the thought of staying in school and communicating with people. I couldn't. Mom's at work, so nobody is home.

I trudge up the stairs, going to my room and falling on my bed.

I hate everything. Hale's words resound in my head, and I can't help but relate to it hard right now.

I'm all ready to fall into a fitful, hibernating sleep but the door bell ringing interrupts me.

Who the hell- I groan when it rings again, pushing myself up and slowly trudging down the stairs.

I peep through the hole, but it's black for some reason. I scowl and opened the door an inch.

"Hey, Rin." I see Evie smiling at me, her hand out stretched probably covering the hole with a finger. "Let me in."

"Evie, I'm really tired." I grumble. "Come back later?"

"No, now." she says, and applies a little pressure on the door. "Rin, I'm not leaving you alone like this. You look ready to jump off a building."

Honest to the core. She really isn't subtle at all.

"What do you want." I whisper, giving in and letting her come in. I don't have the strength to fence off against her anyways.

"Why did you come home early?" she asks, closing the door. She removes her over coat and hangs it, adjusting the scarf around her throat. When I don't answer, she smiles softly and links her arm through mine, leading me to the living room.

"Sit down." she instructs. "I'm going to make some hot cocoa and we're going to have a talk, alright?"

"Okay." I say, not really processing what she is telling me, but letting her do what she wants anyways.

I don't know how long I sit there for, but suddenly she's back, and has a tray with two cups with lids of steam.

"Here you go." she hands me one and takes the other. Placing the tray on the centre table, she sits down next to me and gets comfortable. "Now, tell me what all this is about please."

I remain silent, looking down at the swirls on my coco, the dark chocolate just waiting to be sipped.

"You know you want to." she chides, taking a sip of her own. "Ah, so good. I really do make amazing hot chocolate."
I take a sip to appease her, feeling the warmth run down my body.

"Fine, since you're obviously so adamant to not speak about what happened, let me take a wild guess." she turns her head and looks at me. I am once again struck by her beauty, the way her skin is unblemished and smooth, perfectly wavy, soft blonde hair, bright blue eyes and the way they shine with such kindness and warmth only for the people she loved. For the rest it's stony ice. "Did something happen with the nerd?"

I blink at her, not even surprised that she's figured it out. "I..." I trail off and take another sip. "It isn't my fault, but it feels like it is." I choke.

"Tell me what happened." she says, voice soothing but firm. "You know I always solve your problems." She's right. Ever since we were little, it was always her helping me and Hale finish our school projects, confessing if we ever messed up to our parents, getting us out of detention, making us happy when we were sad.

"I, so Kile tore his pants." I start, because it's lighter and I need to ease into it. "So I went and got him a new pair. He put them on in front of me, which by the way was appalling, and said I had wider hips than him. I told him it was gay, and suddenly he got all serious and offended." I pause to take a deep breathe, drinking more of the warm concoction in my hands. "I asked him why he was getting so offended, and he told me he was..." I have to stop, because I can't say it. "That he..."

"Gay?" she prods, and I shook my head. She looks confused for a second before saying, "...Bisexual?"

I remain silent

"Well, whatever it was, what did you say to that?" she asks, and I feel my fingers trembling again when I recall the scene.

"I-I said that it was wrong, and bad. I told him I could help him-" I put the cup down on the table, and lean forward to bury my fingers in my hair. "I just- I just don't want him to-"

"To what?" Evie asks gently. "Be attracted to guys?"

I nod again.

"Why is it bad?" she asks, sounding genuinely curious. "I'm sorry, Arryn, but I never pegged you to be homophobic."

"I'm not..." I sniff, unsure of my feelings. "Mum says it's wrong."

"She does?" Evie sounds surprised. "Arryn, why do you think being attracted to the same gender is wrong?"

"Because-!" I can't finish. I need to be careful, I can't let her know. "It's unnatural. I mean it's one thing to be... together, but it's a whole other thing to sleep with the same gender. It's gross and horrible."

"And why is that?" Evie puts her own cup of coco down, placing a hand on my shoulder. "Rin, do you think straight sex is horrible?"

"Not really."

"Well, gay sex isn't either. Neither is lesbian sex. Or any other type of sex. Limited to humans." she adds immediately.

"Gay sex hurts." I spit. "It's not normal."

"Well yeah, if you don't prepare it hurts." she explains. "I...don't really know how it works, but any sex would hurt if you don't prepare. Even normal sex will hurt if it's done badly. I mean, do you think rape and sexual assault victims like what's done to them?"

I tense at that, eyes turning moist when I hear that. "What?"

"Hmm?"

"What you- the thing you said. About r..."

Evie blinks and then pulls me to her, hugging me. "I said," she repeats quietly, "That any sexual actions that are forced and unconsented are bad. They hurt, and they're horrible. But when you do it with someone you love, it feels really good." Her cheeks are red, and mine are too. "At least that's what I've been taught through books. And movies."

"But Donna-"

"-is an enigma that we will never figure out." she cuts through. "So yeah. I think you owe an apology to the nerd."

"I think he hates me now." I whisper. "I don't think he ever wants to talk to me again."

"Remember 6th grade, when I accidentally broke that game CD or whatever that you were almost done with?" she says, and I nod. "You screamed at me for an hour, and then chucked me out of your room. I honestly thought that you hated me, and would never want to talk to me again. I thought out friendship was over."

"That's ridiculous." I scoff, a small smile playing on my lips at the memory. It was Uncharted, I think, and I almost finished the game. If she hadn't broken it I would have probably set a new record at how fast I could finish.

"Exactly. I'm sure Kile is also waiting for you to just apologise to him, and make things right." she laughs. "I can bet that he's sitting in his room right now just like you were and wallowing in his own self pity."

"But what about what mom said?" I asks. "She said being gay is bad."

"Don't you have any opinions that your mum disagrees with?" she asks, and I nod.

"She thinks chocolate ice cream is better than chocolate cake." I say. "I like cake better."

"There you go." Evie chuckles. "So now, your mum thinks being gay is bad and you think it's good. Simple!"

"Way to over simplify things." I murmur against her shoulder, and she laughs.

"Life is simple, Rin." she says softly. "If you're ever in a moral dilemma, ask yourself these questions; Does the action affect my life in any way? Does it hurt society or me in any way? And finally, am I willing to give up on our relationship because of this? Trust me, if you answer even two of these questions you'll understand how to proceed further." she said, and kisses my head.

"Wow, I didn't even think of that." I say, frowning slightly when she pulls back and makes me sit straight. "Where are you going?" I ask, when she stands up.

"I have to go back to school, idiot." she huffs, walking to the door. "I was worried so I just dropped by. I still have school."

"What about your coco?" I point to the cup, and she rolls her eyes.

"We both know you'll end up having both." she waves me off, putting her coat on. "I'll text you later, 'kay?"

"Okay." I walk her to the door and watch her move down the porch. "See you later?"

"See you later!" she exclaims, waving as she gets into her car. I watch her car speed off, the Lamborghini glinting under the pale evening sun.

I close the door and go back to the living room. Grabbing the still warm cup of hot chocolate, I pull out the recliner and draw my knees up to my chest.

I have a lot of thinking to do.

12-CHOCOLATE

C hapter 12

Chocolate_______________________

I think about it the whole night. I stay inside my room, just lying down on my bed and thinking.

I, even though Evie talked to me, I'm still conflicted. I still don't know how to approach Kile anymore.

So I go to my reliable helper; Google.

That definitely doesn't help me. Extreme opinions everywhere. I guess I should have expected that, as accepting homosexuality isn't part of the law or anything. It is a personal choice. And what will be mine?

Kile. Honestly, when I first met Kile, I couldn't give a smaller shit about him. The whole tutoring thing was annoying and a stick up my ass if I'm being honest. Kile isn't anything more than a nerd. A goody two shoes. A teacher's pet.

What is it even about him, that I like? I don't know. Is it how he's always happy? Or he always has the goofiest smile when we meet. Or maybe it's his appetite, which is pretty much an endless pit.

The more I think about it, the more I start coming up with new things I love about him.

Are you willing to give up your relationship just because he's attracted to guys?

Of course not. I want to be friends with him forever. I don't want to ditch him. He's almost like Hale and Evie, he's a close friend of mine.

But then I remember what happened that night, and I won't be able to close my eyes without having the flashbacks run through my mind. I hate it. God, I hate it. I hate it so much.

But it isn't fair of me to project my resentment onto Kile. It would be like hating all Mexicans because one Mexican stabbed me.

Logically, I know that Kile didn't do anything wrong, that him being bisexual isn't wrong.

But emotionally it's tough for me to handle. It's tough for me to imagine him with a boyfriend one day, and if I'm being frank, having sex with men. It makes my skin crawl. It makes me feel like throwing up, the idea of someone touching me, the thought of being so vulnerable like that, with no boundaries, with no sort of defense.

But by the morning, I know what my decision is. I know what I have to do, how I actually feel even given the circumstances.

I know I'll never be able to return to being the same old Arryn Donatello, because that boy permanently lost a part of himself that night, on that bed, under him. But I can always try to be that old boy, the golden boy. I know what I have to do; The old Arryn Donatello won't have given a shit if you like boys or girls, because all he cares about is his friends.

And since Kile is a precious friend of mine, I have to apologise and hope he takes me back.

He doesn't come to school the next 2 days.

I wait for him at the top of the steps, but he never shows up. I text him multiple times, and even give in and call him, but he's obviously ignoring me. I wish he would at least read my texts, because I want to apologise.

I went to wait outside the theatre room yesterday for our class, but he never shows up. He really is pissed.

I'm holding off on going and actually meeting him at his house, because I'm, to put it simply, a damned coward. I know I will jumble my words and won't be able to articulate what I want to say properly if we are all alone in his house.

"I can't come for practice today." I tell Hale, as the bell for our final class rings.

"What? Why?" he asks. "Dude, you can't keep doing this. Coach is going to get pissed and I'm running out of cover stories."

"Please?" I beg. "I really need this, Hale. I promise I'll buy you as much pizza as you want tomorrow."

"I'm going to hold you to that." he grumbles, standing up. "Fine. But what do you even need to bunk for?"

"Just math stuff." I say, gathering my things and smiling gratefully at him. "Bye!"

"Hey wait what does that mean?!" He shouts, trying to follow me but tripping over nothing.

"I'll tell you later!" I holler back, before hurrying to my locker downstairs and shoving my books in. Grabbing my back, I grin at Donna, who raises an eyebrow, and jog past her.

Going to my car, I slide in and almost hit some poor girl while reversing. She gives me a terrified look, and I hold a hand up and smile apologetically before driving out of the parking lot.

I know the way to Kile's house by-heart, after all I've been going over for almost 2 weeks now. I sometimes go even when we don't have any classes planned, just because it's fun to be with him.

It comes into view and I park in front of it, behind Kile's own car. Sliding out, I take my bag and fish for the paper I've written my apology on. It's slightly crinkled, but I can still read it just fine.

The nerves in my stomach explode ten fold when I walk up the porch and to the door step. It's quiet, like usual. I waste time in looking at all the plants one by one, before looking back at the door and finally summoning all the courage I have to ring the doorbell.

It rings loudly, and I wait with bated breathe. I'm almost going to ring again but I hear faint foot steps, and suddenly the door swings open.

"Chrissy, I swear to fucking God-" He breaks off, eyes widening in shock and realisation when he sees that it's me. "Arryn?

"Hey Kile." I say, feeling a bit awkward. "Um, did you just take a bath?" I ask, looking at his shirtless body. Minute droplets of water are rolling down his chest, to his hard defined stomach and disappearing down his pants.

"What are you doing here?" he ask coldly, pushing a strand of hair back behind his ear. His hair's wet, sticking to his forehead.

"I- um," I gulp and look down at my feet. "I just, well I wanted to talk to you."

He leans against the door jamb, crossing his arms in front of his chest as he stares at me with no emotion whatsoever.

"Look, I'm busy right now." he says, voice scratchy and hoarse as if he's been shouting or something. "If you're going to stand there quietly then I'll just leave you to it on your own."

"No, wait!" I protest, not wanting him to go yet. "I-" I fumble with the sheet in my hand, feeling my whole face go hot when my eyes blur and I can't read anything. "I'm s-sorry." I stammer, feeling weak, pathetic and angry at myself for being such a fucking coward. "I shouldn't have said that. About you being bisexual. I was...I didn't know better. But now I do and I'm sorry. I hope-" I pause and grab the box of chocolates I bought for him. "I'm so very sorry. I understand if you don't wanna be friends anymore." I choke out before shoving it towards him and turning around to run back to my car and die.

I almost get to the gate before an arm wraps around me and he pulls me back, forcing me to twist around and face him.

"You-" he breaks off, eyes swimming with emotion as he looks down at the box of chocolates and bites down on his lower lip.

"You don't like them?" I ask hurriedly. "They're very good. They're from this super expensive store where mum usually gets sweets for us. So like I thought you might like them since you can never afford them- not that you're poor or anything because you're not I just-" I stop talking because I've dug a grave so deep you can see the centre of the earth.

Kile looks at me in bafflement and wonder, before the most amazing thing happens.

He laughs.

I stare in shock as he throws his head back and laughs loudly, letting go of my arm and clutching his stomach, doubling over.

"F-fuck-" he tries saying something but he bursts out into another set of giggles. I bite my lower lip hard, puffing my cheeks and trying my best to hold the tears in. Is my apology so pathetic that it's this funny?

"I should go." I whisper, and make my way to the car.

"Wait, Arryn!" I grabs me again. "Wait, I'm not angry anymore."

"What?" I ask, whirling around in disbelief.

"I...forgive you." he chuckles. "How could I not after..." he looks down at the chocolates. "I'm sorry too, you know. I think I was a tad dramatic."

"N-No it's fine." I say. What a miracle. To think he would actually forgive me. "Thanks, Kile."

"It's alright." he smiles, the smile that I'm used to and tugs me. "Come in. We'll eat these chocolates together."

"Are you sure?" I ask, resisting his pull. "But, don't you want to eat that with, like, someone else?"

He tips his head to the side, looking confused. "Like who?"

"L-Like a friend-"

"You're a friend." he says. "I want to eat it with you."

"I am?!" I'm incredulous. "Really? You still want to be friends?"

"Uh duh." he says. "Of course. We just had a fight, Arryn. You and I both apologised, so it's in the past now. Don't stress about it, okay?" he smiles, and steps closer, so close that I can smell the shampoo and soap he used for his shower. I just notice that his eyes are red rimmed, and I take his hand.

"Let's eat those chocolates." I smile, and let him lead me into his house. It's as usual, dark and cold, but I can smell a faint scent of perfume.

"Was your mum home or something?" I ask, removing my shoes and stepping in. Kile closes the door and I sigh in relief. "How are you not cold? You shouldn't go outside without at least a t-shirt on, idiot."

"I was in a hurry!" he protests, heading to the stairs. "And no, my mum wasn't home. Why do you ask?"

"Cause it smells like perfume." I tell him, following him upstairs.

"Uh no, that wasn't my mum." he stops at the last step, turning to look at me intently. "It was a girl."

"Oh who?" I ask, wondering why he stopped. I had to lift my neck to look up at him.

"An ex." he says simply, and my eyes widen.

"Oh right, Donna did mention you were kind of a play boy!" I tease, grinning mischievously as he rolls his eyes.

"Nothing happened. She came wanting for a hook-up, that's all."

"Did you?" I ask, pushing forward to resume our walk to his room.

"Hm?"

"Did you hook-up?" I repeat. "Wow, this place is a mess." I comment, walking in and closing the door. "What did you do in here?"

"No, I didn't." he answers the first question. "As for the other one, I tripped over my laundry and fell onto my desk, sending stuff to the floor in my haste to answer the door."

"Sheesh, this wouldn't have happened if you just responded to my texts." I murmur, and he look at me in confusion.

"What texts?" he asks blankly, and I furrow my brows.

"I sent you like a million texts, trying to apologise. Asking to meet up. You didn't see or reply to any." I tell him.

"Oh fuck." he winces, and looks around for something. "I don't even know where my fucking phone is!"

"What?!" I exclaim. "What happened? Did you lose it?"

"I think I was wallowing in my own self pity after what happened, that I completely forgot it existed." he confesses, sitting down on the bed next to me and leaning forward onto his knees. "I don't get any important texts anyways, usually. The only ones I actually looked forward to are yours, and since we, you know, fought and all I didn't expect you to contact me anymore."

He looks so sad and I feel my eyes mist again. I lay a hand on his shoulder, biting my lower lip to keep my emotions in.

"I'm so sorry." I whisper.

"This is going to sound super weird," he laughs dryly, looking down at his hands, "but I kind of really want to hug you right now."

I curse him internally because he's going to make my stupid tears falls.

"It's not all that weird," I sniff, "Because I kind of really want to too."

My last words are muffled against him as he turns around and smothers me in a hug. His arms come around me in a tight embrace, face pressing into my hair as his palms grasp my top tightly. I hug him back, burying my head into the crook of his neck and loving the feeling of his soft, warm skin beneath my fingers. It's still slightly damp from the shower, and his wet hair tickles the side of my face but I don't mind because he's so so comfortable and smells amazing.

"I'm so sorry." I whimper, words getting lost into his skin as I press closer. "I wish I could take that all back." Now that I'm saying it, I'm so glad that I made this decision. It would have been terrible if I ended up losing Kile as a friend.

My hair's wet, and I could tell that he's crying too. "It's okay." his voice is deep and rich. "I was just so sad because you're really important to me and I thought- I didn't even know what I was going to do if we didn't become friends again."

"Me too." I reply. "I don't want us to ever stop being friends."

He slowly pulls back, but just enough so that we're looking at each other. His eyes are wet and red, and I pull a hand up to brush a strand of hair away from his face. He laughs softly and pressed our foreheads together.

"Hi, I'm Kile Dankworth. I'm 18, freshly turned and I love both girls and boys."

I blink at him, and he smiles. I smile back.

"Hi. I'm Arryn Donatello." I say, voice thick. "And I'm fine with that."

His eyes melt and he looks at me in a way, a way that makes my heart go badump.

Badump.

Huh?

I swallow and pull back, placing a hand on my chest. Am I getting a heart attack?

"By the way," I say, and feel a bit confused when he looks away in an unreadable expression. Almost as if he's...disappointed? Deciding that I'm being paranoid, I continue speaking. "By the way, Mrs. Marionette wants to know if you're fine."

"Oh shit." he groans softly. "I'll tell her on Monday. I'll just tell her I was sick or something."

I laugh, lying back against the pillows and fiddling with the strings of my jacket. Kile gets up to grab a t-shirt from his cupboard, slipping it on and coming back.

"Eat the chocolates." I point to the box, and Kile's eyes light up.

"Right, you bought me chocolates." he says, taking the box and then he bursts into a fit of laughter again.

"What?!" I cry, cheeks flaming. "It's an apology...thingie."

"Well, free food so." He shrugs and opens the black satin box. "Gosh, why are rich people so extra."

"I'm not even extra."

"I could buy a 5 books by selling this box." he deadpans, and pops on of the round little brown chocolates into his mouth. A second passes before his eyes bug out and he lets out a long, drawn out moan. I roll my eyes.

"It can't be possible to make chocolate this fucking good." he groans, closing his eyes in agony and bliss.

"I told you." I say simply, smiling as I watch him eat. He soon pops another one in, cheeks darkening in delight.

"You know what, I don't even care if you're the biggest homophobe on this planet as long as you get me these chocolates." he declares, going for a third. "How much did this cost?"

I tell him the price reluctantly and he chokes, hitting his chest to swallow the piece before looking at me with wide eyes.

"I literally don't know how to reply to that." he says blankly.

"Its fine, it's not much for me." I say. "At all." I add, for extra measure.

"I feel like I'm eating diamonds." he says, going for his fifth. "Don't you want one?"

"I'm fine." I deny, looking at him intently. I enjoy the way his face lights up every time he eats, and if I can watch it once more by giving up a chocolate, I'll definitely do it.

"Are you sure? I'll feel bad." he says, and I narrow my eyes.

"Please, you don't feel even an iota of sadness." I scoff.

"Oh, you know me so well." he drawls.

Shaking my head, I kick him and continue to watch him eat.

"Come sit with me." I say suddenly, cutting off whatever story Kile is reciting as we leave the lunch line.

"What?" he asks, blinking at me in surprise.

"Come sit. At my table." I say, nodding in the direction. "I want everyone else to meet you."

"I'm not too sure about that." he tells me, stopping. "I don't think they'll want me to sit with them, Arryn."

"Trust me, they don't give a shit." I argue, linking my arm through on of his and dragging him. "You thought the same about me 50 days back!" I point out, when he tries to resist. "Please? Just give them a chance."

"Okay okay." he grumbles, slackening in my hold and letting me drag him.

"Hey guys." I greet, stopping in front of my table.

"Hey Rin." Evie smiles, scooting over in her seat to make space. I slide down and look up expectantly at Kile, who's still standing there awkwardly.

"Aren't you gonna sit?" Donna asks, taking a bite out of her sandwich. Kile looks surprised at her invite, but graciously takes it and slides in next to me. Opposite us are Donna, Hale and Jason. Peter and some of the other soccer dudes sit a little way off, the cheerleaders with them.

"I think my brain is still stuck in preschool." Hale whines, scrunching his nose. "I hate 12th grade!"

"Same." Jason agrees.

"But you have a fucking soccer scholarship already." Hale points out. "The rest of us have to work."

"I guess." Jason shrugs.

"Is that all you're going to eat?" Evie asks me, scowling at me empty tray, which consists of a single carton of strawberry milk and a banana.

"Yeah, and one sec. Guys. This is Kile. You know him right?" I say, introducing him. "Kile, this is Donna, Jason, Hale and Evie. They're my-"

"Parasites." Hale cuts in. "You're the nerd kid. Giving Rin tuition right?"

"Yep." Kile nods, smiling like the sun. "And you're one of the fastest runners in the team, right?" Hale looks taken aback, and then grins too.

"Yep, you got that right." he snickers. "I'm also the dumbest in this already stupid ass group. Evie is probably the only smart one in this group."

"Hey!" Donna and I say at the same time.

"I guess." Evie agrees. She looks at Kile, and smiles teasingly. "But now, looks like this dweeb is the smartest.

Even though I'm not going to admit it, I sag in relief that Kile got the Evie stamp of approval. If she's okay with it, the whole squad will be. That's just how it works. Queen bee. I chuckle silently to myself.

"Something funny?" Hale, Kile and Evie all ask at the same time, and I do a double take.

"Don't do that, it's creepy." I tell them.

"Do what?" They all say again, and I scrunch my nose.

"Gross." I say, wrinkling my nose.

We talk for the rest of the lunch break. I'm happy to see Kile getting along with everybody, especially Hale and Donna. Evie is kind of quiet the whole time though, playing with her food as she furrows her brows in deep concentration. When I try to ask her if something is up, she denies it but I have this inkling that she's lying to me.

It kind of hurts because Evie usually never lies to me about anything, but again, I would be a hypocrite calling her out on that.

But still, seeing my closest friends getting along with Kile so splendidly makes me really happy, in a way I can't identify. I'm just glad that I can spend more time with him, and the others too.

Even though it's just a 45 minute lunch break, the happiness carries with me to the night.

13-Secrets

C hapter 13

Secrets______________________

"You know what I think?"

"What?" I ask, bored, as I wait for Hale to finish stuffing the pencils into his pouch.

"I think Mickey Mouse would be really good friends with Geronimo Stilton." He says, and I sigh.

"What is your obsession with animated mice?" I ask dryly, walking to the door.

"I'm not obsessed!" he cries, following me closely. "By the way, I completely forgot to tell you."

"What?"

"I have some amazing gossip." he grins like a Cheshire cat, sliding along the marble floor to stop in front of me. I roll my eyes and move him so that I can walk down the stairs.

"Hey!" he catches up, and bounces excitedly. "So, you know Chynna from Junior year yeah?"

"Asian cheerleader who's dating Sandy." I state, stopping in front of my locker. "What happened with her?"

"Right, so the party we had last week - that you didn't come to -" he sends me a dirty look, "there was already this rumour going around that she's been sleeping with Dimitri. Anyways, in the party, some dude got pics of them literally smashing." Hale's cheeks go slightly pink. "She was topless, and on top of him while he-"

"Okay, that's enough." I say, holding my hands up to stop him. "And isn't Dimitri in 10th grade?"

"Yep."

"That's way too young for her to smash, gross." I grimace in disgust. "He's barely 15."

"Yeah, but that's not even the juiciest part!" Hale grins again, jumping from one heel to the other in barely contained excitement. "That asshole uploaded the pictures online, through her Instagram account!"

"What?" I asked, perplexed. "How is that even-"

"- possible? I don't know man, but he somehow got access to it or something - or she - and uploaded those pictures as her latest posts and story." He presses his lips together. "Her mother follows her."

"Holy shit." I wince. "Fuck, that couldn't have gone down well."

"Her family is pretty conservative." Hale nods. "Like her parents not much, but all her cousins, aunts and uncles found out. They're pulling her out of this school."

"Holy crap, that's crazy." I say, and Hale nods.

"What's crazy?" Evie yawns, appearing from down the hallway and stopping in front of us. "Shit, I'm so sleepy."

"Chynna is getting pulled out." Hale explains, and I let Evie lean on my shoulder.

"Yeah I heard." Evie yawns again. "Right, I saw those pictures. I was checking my feed in front of mom, can you even believe it. And that picture popped up. At least it was taken down after all her friends reported it and it was uncensored nudity anyway."

"But the damage was already done." Hale shrugs. "And I-"

"HALE MIRELLA!" Someone screams, and the entire corridor goes silent. Hale jerks from surprise, and I look down the hallway in confusion to see a girl and her gang of bitches furiously making their way down right to us.

"Um Hale." Evie asks quietly. "What did you do man."

"What are you-" he whirls around and his eyes widen in what I could only describe as terror. "Oh fuck."

"What did you do, dude." I press, eyes widening with every step the girl takes to us. I recognise her vaguely, I think she is part of the disciplinary committee, if I'm not mistaken. She has black curly hair and was short, quite pretty. But she looks seriously frightening with that ugly snarl and her spiky, leather boots.

"Betty." Hale chokes out, when she reaches us. There are three girls behind her, all wearing similar expressions of anger and disgust, hands on their hips. Betty is so small, that in front of Hale, Evie and I she looks like a frog.

"Hale, you fucking son of a bitch!" she screams, high voice piercing through my ear drums.

"Woah, what the hell?" I say, when she takes a threatening step forward. "Betty, calm down."

"Shut the fuck up!" she screeches, and pushes me violently. I'm pushed back into Evie, who thankfully catches me. I feel a spark of fear course through me when she turns to me with her insane eyes, and even though she is half my height I still felt myself shrivel when her eyes narrow, fingers flexing. I'm so pathetic, how can I get scared of this pesky girl who barely reaches my shoulder? I can't even move, slagging against Evie, the events of that night flashing through my eyes as quick as light, but I force myself to shut it down.

Betty grab Hale by his collar, and when I see his expression, I can't move. I've never seen him look so terrified in my life. Who is this girl and what did she do to him that is making him so scared?

"Betty-"

"Don't fucking say my name!" She slams him against the locker violently, and he lets out a pained groan as the back of his head hits the hard metal.

"Betty stop!" A familiar voice has me looking to the side and seeing Kile, trying to push his way to the front of the crowd.

"You're a fucking loser, you disgusting piece of trash!" she slaps Hale across the face, her nails leaving red streaks across his tanned skin.

"Get away from him-" My yell is cut short when Evie moves from behind me and grabs Betty by the hair, swinging her around and slamming her back into the locker.

"Bitch, how dare you?" Evie growls, and raises a hand to punch her. I shoot forward, Kile at the same time, and we both catch her hand before she nails that girl's face in.

"Evie calm down!" I cry, when she tries to pull her hand back. I can hear someone screaming to get a teacher.

"She pushed you, she fucking hit Hale-"

"I know." I stop her. "But-" I'm cut short when Betty pushes Evie back.

"I only did what that fucking faggot deserved." she spits. I look at her in shock, and Hale makes a noise akin to a wounded animal. "You couldn't even get it up for me, you disguising flaming homo!"

Evie reels back in, but Kile catches her around the waist and hauls her back.

"Hale!" I shout when he turns and bolts, running from us and pushing through the crowd.

"Wait!" I look at Evie and Kile, and he nods before tightening his hold on Evie when she lunges for Betty again, and I take off after him. I don't know what's wrong, but I do now that I can't leave Hale alone after what just happened.

"Damn it, he's fast." I grit out, chasing after him, hot on his trail as Hale barrels through the back door and runs to the field.

I forgot that he is one of the fastest runners on the team, but even he has an ending point. He starts slowing down before jumping behind the seats in the bleachers, disappearing.

I slow down too, panting at the run I just had.

"Fuck, my legs." I exhale, walking down the field as I make my way to where he's slipped through.

"Hale?" I call out softly, ducking under the metal bars to reach him.

"Hale?" I repeat, sliding in. It's a small area of grass, and the rows of seats above us let in slits of pale sunlight. Hale is sitting against one of the poles, curled into a ball and rocking back and forth.

"Hale." I call out softly. "Shit, are you alright?"

He doesn't reply.

"It's only me, Hale." I look down at the grass for a second before carefully lowering myself down. I sit down with my legs folded, opposite to him so that he is facing me.

"Please look up." I whisper. "Betty is a bitch."

"But what she said was true!" Hale finally speaks, and he sounds awful. The words are thick, and his voice grating. He is crying.

"What was true?" I ask, and he slowly looks up. I feel my heart break at his red, puffy eyes, tear streaked cheeks and running nose. "Come here." I say, and pull down my sleeve so that I can wipe his eyes and nose. "Hale, what was she talking about?"

Hale looks at me silently, and then closes his eyes tightly.

"Shit." he curses. "Arryn, I don't want you to hate me."

"What?" I ask, perplexed. "I could never hate you, Hale."

"You never know."

"Yes, I do. Now tell me."

He remains silent for a while longer, but then his expression hardens and he looks at me.

"I've not told anyone this." he whisper. "The only one who probably knows is Evie. She's way too smart for her own good. But I know that she's fine with it."

"What is it?" I ask again. "Hale, whatever it is I want you to know that you'll still be my best friend."

"I-" he turns away. "Rin...I think, I think...I'm gay."

I blink at him, utterly and completely taken aback.

"Oh." I whisper.

"Oh? That's it?" he asks dryly, when I don't say anything else.

"No! Um," I'm fumbling for words. "Congratulations."

"Thanks." he deadpans, and then exhales shakily. "Do you care? D-Does it matter?"

"No, it doesn't." I shake my head. "O-Of course not. Hale, it doesn't matter at all."

"So we're still best friends?" he chokes out, and I nod.

"Of course." my voice cracks slightly. "Always."

"Wow, I thought Hale was going to be crying. Didn't think it would be the both of you." We both turn and see Evie ducking in. She tucks in her skirt and sits down on the grass.

"You're eyes are red too." I accuse, only then realising that my eyes are wet. "Were you crying?

"No I wasn't." she mumbles adamantly. "So Hale, I got Betty expelled."

"What?!" We both exclaim, and she smiles tiredly.

"Pulled some strings. We won't be seeing her again." she exhales. "She's also going to be attending a camp teaching diversity and equality. Courtesy to me."

"Evie, you're amazing." Hale chokes out, and Evie crawls forward to wrap her hands around him.

"I don't know what she was on about." Evie whispers. "But it isn't true."

"I'm gay." Hale says. "We were going to hook up last Friday's party. But I couldn't...you know."

"I know." Was all Evie says, before sitting back. "Thank you for telling me." she grins wickedly. "I'll try to keep the dirty dirty dreams I have of us at bay-"

"Gross!" Hale and I shout, covering out ears. Evie laughs loudly, and shakes her head.

"We're all still best friends right?" Hale asksd. "We'll always be together, no matter what."

Evie and I exchange a glance before saying, "No matter what."

We are all silent, and I look down at the grass, fiddling with the small green strands.

Evie and Hale are my best friends. We've grown up together, and even when Hale moves]d away for half a year or I had to go to my father's place all summer, we never let go. We always remained friends. Our bond is strong.

I feel bad that I'm keeping a secret then, all to myself when Hale has told us his biggest secret. I want to tell them, but at the same time I don't. I don't know how that is possible, but on one hand I can't bare the vulnerable position I'll be in when I disclose something like that. But on the other hand, my mental state is pretty much a lump of clay, my rape molding and testing it in anyway it can. I don't know how much longer I can go with holding it in, holding it all inside. Shadows in my own damn room still make me jump, even after a whole month. In the night I either don't sleep or get nightmares. I can't sleep on my side because I'm too scared that someone will come and hurt me from my back.

I hate how weak I am. I hate how I don't have the mental endurance to even fucking take a bath without locking the door. I despise how if anybody I don't know even touches me slightly, it sends shivers down my back. I hate it all, and I want it to stop.

The three of us go back to the school building. Kile is waiting for us at the back exit, leaning against the glass doors.

"She's gone." he says, when we reach him. "Gosh, I don't believe she created such a ruckus just because you didn't sleep with her."

"I'm gay." Hale announces. "I'm gay, that's why I didn't sleep with her."

Kile looks taken aback, and Evie laughs.

"You don't have to announce it to everybody, Hale." she says, sounding amused. "Unless you want to."

"Well, I'm bisexual so I don't really care." Kile shruggs, his eyes flitting up to me at that. I smile at him encouragingly and he licks his bottom lip, eyes narrowing.

"Oh." Hale blinks. "That's nice."

"I want to talk to you for a sec." Kile says, looking directly at me. "Evie, I hope you've calmed down."

"Yeah yeah." she makes a disgusted face. "And it's Evette to you, mister."

She takes Hale's hand in her own and walks forward with him, holding her other hand up as a wave.

"Hey, what's up?" I ask, when we are left alone.

"Follow me." he orders, grasping my hand. I flinch and he lets go, looking at me with an unreadable expression before walking to one of the doors. It is an empty classroom, probably only used by the art club twice a week.

"What is it?" I ask, closing the door behind me. I feel really bad that I flinched at Kile's touch. It isn't him I am afraid of, but my head space isn't the best right now.

"I just wanted to know if you're okay." he steps up to me until we are face to face, his proximity making me lean back slightly. "You were scared right?"

"Huh?" His hand lifts up slowly, and he pauses at my face, eyes questioning me. When I don't object, he places it on my cheek before slowly moving it down to my neck. Goosebumps erupt over my skin, and I inhale sharply. What is happening? Why am I reacting like this?

"I wasn't scared." I say, trying to gain back my awareness.

"I saw you. When she pushed you." Kile steps forward and his eyes flash in anger. "That stupid bitch. I saw you internally freak out. I'm so sorry, Rin." The use of my nickname sends my cheeks red, and he presses his lips together.

"I just felt that you really needed a hug." he says, and wraps his arms around me, warm body flush against mine. I gasp softly, automatically folding into him as one arm goes around my waist and the other to the back of my head to push it onto his shoulder.

My fingers trembled, but not because I'm scared, and I hesitantly wrap them around him, sliding them up the expanse of his back. I press my face into the crook of his neck, liking how he squeezes me even tighter.

This is so weird. Were his shoulders always this broad?

"Idiot, you don't have to be sorry for anything." I mutter against his warm neck, blushing when I feel his mouth run past my ear.

"If I'd just gotten there sooner-"

"It was not in your control." I cut him. "Stop blaming yourself. I'll get mad."

"Mad? You will?" Kile laughs and pulls back slightly. I immediately miss his warmth, but let him step back so that we can look at each other.

"Mhm." I look at him silently before saying, "Actually, I want to thank you."

"Thank me?" he echoes, tipping his head to the side curiously.

So cute.

What.

"Yeah." I say, looking down to where his arms are still wrapped loosely around my hips. "For just...you know, if I'd never met you, then I probably would have gone all freaked out on Hale and...I'm just glad that you were there to knock some sense into me before."

"Your welcome." he grins, and steps back completely, our arms falling down from each other's bodies. I rub my arms with my palms, because I am suddenly cold.

I will never tell him this to his face, but I'm really glad I met Kile. We didn't exactly start off on a great foot, and frankly speaking the Arryn from 2 months ago would probably be mortified that I'm hanging out with him, but I don't care.

Funny how things work themselves out sometimes.

14-reminiscence

C hapter 14

Reminiscence _______________________

I think my eyes just spontaneously combust as I see Hale walk into school with a bright, rainbow coloured t-shirt and the weirdest looking pants I've ever seen. Evie's hand slips and the water from the water bottle spills all over her.

"Jeez, are you okay?" I ask, as she doubles over in raucous coughs and sputters.

"Please poke out my eyes with a hot iron bar." she says between her coughs.

"Only if you do mine first."

"This is all your fault you know." Evie says, standing back up and wiping her wet mouth. "You're responsible for this."

"Don't look at me, he's your son." I retort, grimacing as his t-shirt catches the light and actually blinds me this time.

"Hey guys!" he exclaims, a shit-eating grin on his face. "How are you this gay morning?"

"I've been scheduled for a pupil retraction surgery." Evie says.

Hale's grin grows wider.

"You know what, I love being gay." he says, nodding. "Like love it. Ahh, it's so good to be living my truth-"

"Please stop, I physically can't take it anymore." I protest weakly, trying not to look anywhere down his face. "Gosh, Hale. Why are you like this?"

"You even got my shirt all wet." Evie snorts, wiping her now translucent white tank top with a hand kerchief. "Shit, I don't have an extra top."

"U-Um-"

The three of us look to see a boy standing a little way off, staring at us. He has brown, messy hair and black glasses. His face is slightly red, and he's holding out something.

"What do you want?" Evie and Hale ask at the same time.

"I-I'm Jamie! We're Biology partners, if you forgot." his voice trails off to the end. "I um, your shirt," he goes pink, "I can see inside-"

"Bad day to wear a neon pink bra, dude." Hale whistles, and Evie glares at him.

"I'll just have to wait for it to dry, I don't have anything else. I left my jacket at home." she says, and then glares at a passing group of boys who shamelessly ogle her breasts.

"Fuck off." I snap at them, and they run away down the hall. I'm offering her one of my tops when the boy speaks again.

"I have, um, an extra t-shirt." The boy - Jamie - squeaks. "Please take it."

Evie blinks at him. "It won't fit me."

"What?" Jamie asks, looking surprised.

"Your top." Evie explains. "I'm like half a foot taller than you."

"And she has humongous boobs-" Hale yelps when I step on his foot.

"You're not h-half a foot taller than me!" Jamie exclaims, voice high and indignant. "It's barely 2 inches! And I'm still growing."

"Thanks Jamie, but Rin here already has a hoodie I can borrow." she smiles, and Jamie blushes all the way to the tips of his ears.

"Yep. I was just going to give it to you." I say, turning to my locker.

"Oh, okay." Jamie shoulders sag a bit. "I, um, I'm glad you have something to wear."

"Thanks again. See you in bio!" she calls out, and he nods furiously before bounding back down the hallway.

"Wow, Evie, that guy totally has the hots for you." Hale laughs, and Evie frowns at him as she takes the extra hoodie from me.

"No he doesn't." she pauses. "I'm pretty sure he's gay, anyways."

"Really?" Hale asks, looking interested. "But still, kinda brave of him to offer you clothes right in front of your boyfriend."

"Hm?" Evie says, and I look at him in confusion.

"What do you-" I stop, and Evie clamps a hand over her mouth when Hale turns to us with confused looks.

"What?" he says, and I shake my head.

"N-Nothing." Evie replies too, cheeks a little pink. "But yeah, I don't think he meant any harm.

"Yeah." I say. "And it didn't feel offensive anyways. Like he was just trying to help Evie. My girlfriend."

Evie and I share a glance, and then immediately look away. Hale continues chattering some nonsense as we walk down the hall to our classes.

But all I can think of is how I forgot that Evie and I are dating.

I don't believe we both forgot that we're dating.

"Bye, see you after class." Evie says, when we reach the stairs.

"Yeah, bye." Our eyes meet for a second, and we both look away at the same time.

It's weird. Evie and I are super close, things are never awkward between us. Even though she is a girl, and I'm a boy, it doesn't really matter to us. We change in front of each other, sleep over randomly, and even our parents don't care if we lock ourselves in a room together.

I still remember the day I asked Evie out.

It was the beginning of 11th grade, and we were at some party, like usual. I'd remembered Jason, Gary and some of my other team mates teasing me about my relationship with Evie. Until then, I'd never considered ever dating her, but when Peter said that it would probably happen anyways, since we were the most popular people in school, I decided to just ask her out.

So I went up to her and asked her if she wanted to be my girlfriend. Probably not the best timing, considering what she had been doing at that time.

"Evie?" I called out, walking out of the house to the back yard. "You there?"

"Yeah, here!" I heard her muffled voice, and followed it until I reached her.

"What on earth are you doing?" I asked, looking at her as she was in a hand stand, a cake below her.

"I was challenged." she said, voice muffled and face covered with chocolate. "Hale told me I could never finish a chocolate cake upside down."

"What is it with you and Hale always at each other's throats?" I laughed, walking to her and sitting on a bench. "Well, I just wanted to ask you if you wanted to be my girlfriend."

"Girlfriend?" she echoed, and I nodded. "Why?"

"Because everyone is saying it'll happen anyways, and they're expecting it since we're the most popular people in school." I explained. "I guess it makes sense."

"Don't you go out with someone who you are in love though?" Evie asked, doing a slight hand stand pushup to take another bite out of the cake.

"I guess. I don't know. I love you though." I said. "Do you love me?"

"Yeah." she replied. "Hmm. Oh, how about...if I finish this cake I'll go out with you."

"Really?" I asked, and she awkwardly did a hand-stand nod.

"Yeah. One sec." she said, and I watched her as she ate the entire cake, and then rolled forward with a loud sigh.

"Aaah, that was amazing!" she said, lying flat on her back with her hands spread out. "Okay, I guess I'll become your girlfriend."

"Nice!" I exclaimed, and slid down onto the grass so that I was lying down next to her. "So, should we like do something?"

"Something like what?"

"Like kiss, or I don't know. To commemorate out newly formed relationship."

"Uh, okay." she rolled over until she was straddling me, hands on either side of my face. Her blonde hair was tied up in a bun, but a few wisps fell down, framing her beautiful face.

This position reminded me of the wrestling match we'd had last weekend. I'd won 3, she won 2.

"Hey, this reminds me that I still have to win a match against you." she said, and I laughed.

"I was literally thinking the same thing." I said, and closed my eyes for the kiss.

She leaned down and pressed her lips to mine softly.

Oh shit I forgot to buy Mika pudding.

She pulled back and rolled off of me. "Guess we're dating now."

"Yeah, I guess."

"Doesn't that sound like a sister?"

I blink at Kile, the fork stopped halfway to my mouth.

"What?" I ask, and he shrugs, leaning on one hand.

"Well, it seems like that relationship is one between siblings." he explains. "I'm an only child, so I can't tell indefinitely, but- okay, just imagine this. If Evie was a boy and 6 years younger than you, wouldn't she basically be Mika?"

I feel the piece of apple fall from my mouth and onto the table with a thud.

"Holy- Holy fucking hell." I say, everything becoming clear all of a sudden. "Holy shit. Holy fuck. Holy Guacamole."

"So, are you going to break up with Evie?" Kile asks, shifting on the chair. His t-shirt slides down one shoulder, and I look away.

"I...don't know." I say unsurely, and Kile hums.

"Are you sure you don't want anything else?" He asks, gesturing to my plate. "I have cake, if you want."

"I'm good, thanks." I say. "Hey, can we go up to your room?"

"Yeah sure." he nods, taking my plate even though I protest and dropping it into the sink.

"I could have done that myself." I murmur, following him upstairs to his room.

"You're a guest. It's basic cordiality." he grins, opening the door and holding it for me.

A smile lifts the corners of my lips when I smell his scent in the room. Something about Kile's scent is comforting, like a warm blanket. I especially love it when he hugs me. And he hugs me a lot.

"Are we going to do math now?" I ask, bouncing on his bed. "By the way, aren't you proud of the marks I got in the last class test?"

"Immensely proud." he says, sliding in next to me, nudging me so that we're sitting side by side. I yawn, feeling my eyes droop. "How come you're always tired?"

"I don't get much sleep usually." I say truthfully. "Barely 4 hours if I'm lucky." I don't tell him why though.

"Shit, that sucks." he says. "Do you want to sleep now?"

I laugh at that. "No way! I don't want to sleep on this small ass bed."

"It's normal, you just have a humongous bed." he snorts. "I'd actually quite like to see it."

"Then come over some time." I blurt without thinking. Wait, shit. Bringing someone to my room? I haven't even had my best friends in my room for over a month. My room's my safe space. I don't know how I'll react to Kile coming inside there. Would it be okay?

"Really?" I turn to him at the excitement in his voice. "I can? I'm so excited."

"Yeah..." I say, because I can't very well take the offer back now. But somehow, seeing his pumped face makes me smile; maybe it won't be so bad to have him come over after all.

"So, back to the previous topic." Kile interrupts my thoughts. "Are you breaking up with Evie?"

"I have no idea." I answer. "But...maybe? I'm not sure. I'll talk to her, definitely. Maybe I am in love with her, I just don't know it."

Kile doesn't say anything, and I almost thought he's asleep but he suddenly turns around and presses his face into my chest, hugging me tightly.

"What happened?" I ask, running my fingers softly through his fluffy hair.

"Nothin'." He mumbles against my body, not looking up at me. "Yo.r..ot..lo..er."

"What?"

"Nothing." he says, and looks up at me, chin braced on my sternum. "When can I come over?"

"Anytime." I shrug. "We can go tomorrow. Since I don't have prac-tice."

"Why not?"

"The fields are too wet because of the rains. I think like 5 people have already fallen and sprained their ankles." I say. "So we have this week off."

"I see." he softly traces a pattern on my arm over my jacket sleeve. "I can't wait till tomorrow."

"Me neither, Kile."

I leave a little while after that. I don't know whether I should wait till tomorrow to talk to Evie or not, but decide to just go for it and talk to her today itself. Best to get it over with.

I pull my car up in front of her drive way, and park it. Leaving my bag in the car, I jog through the slight drizzle up her porch and knock on the door.

I wait for a few minutes before it opens and I'm met with a boy. "Hey Laurent." I greet. Laurent Wilson is Evie's twin younger brother. He has orangish brown hair, which is actually their natural hair colour but Evie dyes hers blonde for some reason.

"Hey Rin. Come in." he says, brushing his hair out of his eyes. I know that Laurent doesn't attend school, he's already in college, has been since last year. He's almost as tall as me, but will probably surpass me since his dad is fucking huge.

"Is Evie there?" I ask, and he nods.

"Yeah, she should be upstairs. I think she was doing her homework." he says, as we walk down the foyer to the hall. "Is something the matter?"

"Not really." I say, stopping. "Just have something to talk about. I'll catch you later, okay?"

'Yeah, see you." he nods, before shuffling back to the kitchen to resume whatever he was doing. I go up the stairs, heading to her room.

"Hey Evie." I open the door and pop in.

"Oh hey." she says, looking up from where she's doing something on her laptop on the bed. "What's up? Just one sec."

"Watcha doing?" I ask, closing the door and making my way to her, sitting down next to her.

"It's just Jamie." she says, typing something. "We're lab partners and stuff, so we were just discussing project details. I'll tell him that I'll talk to him later."

"Is the project hard?" I ask, and she nods, typing a few last words before shutting her laptop.

"Yeah kinda. But it's also fun." she shrugs. "So what's up. Why're you here?"

"I just..." I turn her way so that I can look at her seriously. "Hey, so it wasn't just me who forgot that we were dating, right?"

She shifts slightly, chest rising slowly as she breathes, bottom lip being worried by her teeth.

"No it wasn't." she finally says. I'm going to speak, but she cuts me off. "Hey, Rin, can I be completely honest here?"

"Yeah, sure." I ask. "You can tell me anything."

She nods. "So like, aren't you in love with Kile?"

"What?" The reply is rapid, harsh and high. She looks at me with a sympathetic expression, and I just want to tell her to stop it because she obviously doesn't know what she is talking about. Where did that even come from? "Evie, stop talking nonsense. Kile and I are friends."

"I know." she says. "I mean, I can see that. You were friends."

"Are friends."

"Rin, has it ever occurred to you that, that what you two do together isn't something...normal friends would do?" she says hesitantly, as if she's afraid I will burst.

"What does that even mean?" I snap, glaring at her. "We're just close friends."

"Rin, we're the bestest friends that can be and I still don't hug you everyday. Hell, I don't think I hug you every 3 days." she says. "I've seen you both...when you think you're alone. Jesus, Rin, that guy can't keep his hands off of you."

"That's not true." I defend. "Kile's just an affectionate person. Are you saying a man can't be affectionate? That's sexist, Evie."

"You know very well that's not what I'm saying!" her eyes flash and I can tell she's getting irritated. "You know what, drop it. You won't listen anyways."

"I'm not listening because there's nothing going on!" I exclaim. "We're just close friends."

"Alright alright." she shakes her head. "I concede. You're just close friends. Is there anything else you wanted to talk about?"

"No."

"Then leave. I still have my project to do." she says.

"I can't believe you're kicking me out because of this!" I say, and she sighs.

"I'm not kicking you out." she says, and then leans forward to wrap her arms around me. "I'm not angry. I actually have a lot of work to do."

"Okay fine." I mumble, hugging her back. Kile's hugs are warmer...

"You just thought something along the lines of 'Kile's hugs are warmer', right?"

"I'M LEAVING!" I yell, pushing her away and leaving her laughing on her bed as I go.

15-SLEEP

"**Y**our house is huge!"

I gave him a disgusted look and pushed him forward, up the porch steps.

"It's just a regular house." I said, taking out my keys to unlock the door.

"This house is as big as 3 of my house." Kile sniffed, following me inside. "What do you even need such a big house for is my question. Your parents must be insanely rich."

"Just my mom, actually." I said, closing the door and removing my coat. "My dad isn't around anymore."

"Divorced?"

'Yeah. Left like 10 years back."

"Shit, that sucks." Kile said.

"It's fine. I don't really care anymore." I assured him, leading him down the foyer to the hall. "It was a long time ago."

"Do you still meet him?" Kile asked, looking star struck as he took in the couches of the living room, and I had to urge him to sit on them.

"Not very often. Mika and I usually go over summer to where he stays, to meet our grand parents and stuff. We're pretty close to them since mom's parents died before we were born." I threw my bag carelessly on one sofa, joining him on the love seat. "What about your parents? I don't think I've seen them even once when I came over."

"Yeah, they're not around very much." Kile said, his expression far away. "They're kind of workaholics, so they leave me alone at home a lot since they have business trips and stuff."

"Since when have they been leaving you alone?" I asked, and Kile shrugged.

"Ever since I came to high school. They said I was old enough. It's why I cook really well." Kile smiled crookedly at me. "One day, you should come over for dinner and I'll cook for you."

"That sounds awesome." I said, grinning. "Speaking of food, you want anything right now?"

"I'm not hungry." Kile said, but then his stomach growled loudly and he blushed, making me raise an eyebrow at him.

"I think we have some lasagna from last night, ohh, and there's pita bread and hummus." I told him, dragging him off the sofa even though he protested and leading him to the kitchen. "We can even make some sandwiches. Or we can order food. Pizza, or-"

"I think lasagna is fine." Kile interrupted.

"Alright." I conceded. "Can you grab two forks? I'll heat it up and then we can go up to my room."

"Why are forks so fucking fancy." he groaned, and I ignored him as I rummaged through the fridge for the glass casserole.

"Pepsi or Sprite?" I asked.

"Pepsi, please. And I got the forks. I think the lasagna's done." I heard the ding of the microwave, and Kile opening the door. I went to the cabinet above the counter and grabbed two glasses.

"I should have asked the cook to come down today." I said, as we both head to the stairs. "He could have made us something nice."

"Nah that's fine- wait, you have a cook?!" he yelped when I elbowed him, sticking out his tongue and running up the steps.

"Careful, you'll drop the forks." I called after him.

"Which room is yours?" he asked, looking at the stretch of doors down the corridor.

"This one." I said, nodding in its direction. " The one next to it is Mika's. Mom's right opposite."

"Wow, for such a big house you have only 3 bedrooms?" he asked, and I shook my head.

"On the opposite side, we have rooms which we converted into a den and a study for mom when she needs to work late. We broke down the wall between 2 rooms to make the den."

"That's amazing." Kile walked up to my room and waited expectantly.

"I sweat to god if you make some foolish comments..." I opened the door, a tad hesitant, and held in a sigh when he gasped dramatically.

"Son of a biscuit! To think, TO THINK, you've been living in such luxury-!"

"It's not even that big." I said, kicking the door closed and following him as he pranced around everywhere.

"I bet this carpet costs more than my life." He said, running his toes through the soft carpet.

"Stop being dramatic and help me with all this stuff." I ordered. He took the casserole from my hand and bounced on the bed, scooting his butt to bury himself in it comfortably. I swallowed and looked back at the door. Should I have closed it? I shouldn't have closed it.

Stop being foolish. It's Kile. The most harmless, nice and genuine person you know. He won't do anything.

I hated myself so much for it, but I found my eyes roaming the room for my phone and baseball bat.

Just incase.

"Aren't you going to sit?" Kile asked, and I was broke out of my betraying thoughts by him. I blinked down at him, and he smiled, patting the spot next to him.

Immediately I felt a little relieved. I was being overly paranoid. Kile wouldn't do anything. He was kind, and fun, and handsome-

"Woah." It slipped out of my mouth before I could control it, and Kile gave me an odd look.

"Are you alright? Do you have to poo?"

"No, I don't have to poo." I said dryly, feeling at ease again as he teased me. I sat down beside him, pressing against the headboard and sighing in relief when I sank into the fluffy pillows.

"Ah, this feels good." I said. "School today was so tiring."

"We still have 2 days for weekend, though." Kile whined, laying his head on my shoulder as he stabbed the lasagna and took a bite. "Mmn, yummy. It's even better than what I make."

"My mom made it." I said. "I can ask her to tell you the recipe. When she comes back home."

"That'll be great." Kile mumbled. "You know what, I agree. My bed's trash compared to yours."

"Mmh, yeah." I answered softly, because everything felt soft right now. "Hey, Kile, do you like anyone right now?"

"Hm? Like?"

"Yeah. Like. Like, like like." I explained, and he laughed softly.

"That's a lot of likes." he paused, shifting. "Maybe."

"Really?" I was mildly surprised. "Who is it? Is it someone I know?"

"Maybeee." he repeated, and I pouted, wondering why he was being so vague.

"Tell me. Atleast tell me if it's a boy or girl." I pleaded, and he chuckled.

"Okay. It's a boy."

"Woah." I felt myself brush a little, and suddenly my chest felt a little heavy, a familiar but unwelcome tug emanating through my ribs. "Um, who is it?"

"Not telling."

"Please? I won't tell anyone."

"Nope!"

"At least describe him?" I persisted, and he sighed before nodding against me.

"Alright. He's tall-"

"How tall?" I cut in.

"About as tall as me." Kile said. "He has really nice hair, and the most beautiful eyes I've ever seen."

"What's he like?"

"At first I thought he was annoying." Kile said. "But then we became friends, and I've come to really love him. He's funny, and really nice when you get to know him. Most people think he's a dick though."

"Oh. So, does he go to our school?" I pressed.

"I don't know." I could hear his grin. "He's really stupid though, sometimes. I've tried dropping hints like crazy but he never gets them. And there are these moments where I feel like he's hiding something, and these other times when he looks really, really sad or scared. I just want to hug him tightly and lock us together in a room so that nobody can hurt him."

"Wow, you must really like this guy." I said, playing with his hair. I wonder if he would ever like me.

"Excuse me." I said, and pushed him gently to get off the bed.

"Where are you going?" he asked, as I made my way over to the bathroom.

"One sec, have to pee." I told him, and closed the bathroom door behind me before walking to the wall and bashing my head against it.

Idiot idiot idiot idiot. I scolded myself, going to the sink and turning the tap all the way to the cold side before dunking my head under it. Stop thinking weird things. It's just Evie messing with you.

I waited till I wasn't gritting my teeth against the cold anymore before switching off the water. Quit thinking stupid stuff like this. Kile would never like you. Even if he did, he shouldn't. You're used and gross, leftovers that nobody wants.

Slapping my cheeks three times, I took a breathe before walking back to the door and rubbing my hair with the towel hanging there.

I opened it and stepped out, pausing when I saw that Kile was stretched out on my bed. I stopped walking and looked at him, feeling a small smile pinch my cheeks when he lightly snored. He'd fallen asleep waiting for me.

I resumed my walk and went up to him, unfolding my comforter before dragging it over him, making sure he was completely covered. I removed the casserole and other food items, placing them on my desk before going back to the bed. Climbing onto it, I sat beside him and stared down at him, taking in the features of his face. I'd never seen him up close like this, still and laid out for me.

He really was pretty, it was a shame he masked it behind glasses and his nerdiness. I realised then that he was wearing his glasses, so I gently plucked them out and placed them on my night stand. Without his glasses, he looked much better.

I slid down the bed and lay down on my side, curling my knees to my chest as I continued to watch him sleep. He looked really tired, for some reason. He had eye bags, and his skin was paler than usual. My gaze dropped to his lips, and I was enamoured by the delicate curves, the soft cuts and dips of the pink flesh, plump and slightly pouted as he breathed softly.

I didn't realise until my eyes were already half closed that my breathing had started to match his, but by the time I could do anything about it I was already in the darkness and falling asleep.

"RING RING RING RING RING RING RING RING RING RING RING-"

"What the hell?"

I was woken up by someone cursing and an annoying noise in the background disrupting my ears.

"W-Wha-" I mumbled incoherently, wondering what was happening as my tired eyes fought to open against the heaviness and lethargy. It took me a moment to register it was morning, and I was going to roll over to switch off my alarm, but something prevented me.

I made a small noise and looked down, and then I was suddenly wide awake.

"Kile?!" I exclaimed, lifting the covers slightly to get a full view of him. Fucking hell, the guy was still fast asleep (not asleep enough to curse though), and he was tightly hugging me around the torso, his face literally pressed into my stomach. "Kile, wake up."

"Mmnm." he groaned, shifting so that he pressed further against me, and I flushed, frantically trying to pry him off.

"Stop being a baby and get off!" I scolded, and he just mumbled something dumb again.

Holy shit holy shit holy fucking shit Kile is sleeping in my bed and he's cuddling- Oh my god I don't believe we slept all through evening to the night- oh my god I don't believe I actually slept for more than 4 hours-

I decided to push my confusing thoughts to the side because if my alarm clock was ringing, it meant that it was almost 8 in the morning and we were going to be late.

"Kile, we're going to be late for school." I tried. "We need to get to school, you hear? Wake up."

"Ughhh, okay." he grumbled, finally pushing his head back to look at me. "G'Morning." he grinned, bed hair messy and cheeks pink.

"I don't believe we just slept off like that." I said, probably still blushing as I finally managed to peel him off of me and slide off the bed. I switched off my alarm clock and had my second heart attack of the day.

"Shit, it's 8:15 Kile! You're gonna miss first period." I said, feeling horrible because Kile didn't like to miss classes and I'd made him sleep past time.

"It's fineee." Kile said, pushing himself up slowly and rubbing one eye. "With my record, I'd be okay if I bunked school for a whole week."

"We still need to go though." I mumbled, walking to my bathroom. "Come on, I have an extra toothbrush."

"Why do you have an extra toothbrush?" he asked, following me.

"I just always keep one. Incase I need to change it." I told him, leaving the door open and grabbing mine. I ducked down and opened the cabinet door, taking out another brush for him. "Here."

"Wouldn't your mum have woken you up?" Kile asked, putting paste on the bristles before shoving it into his mouth. He knocked me with his hip to make me move, so that we could both see ourselves in the mirror.

"Nah, if I don't wake up myself by like 7:30, she usually assumes I'm bunking or something." I said, words muffled by my toothpaste filled mouth. "Won't your parents be mad that you stayed over here?"

"I don't think they're even home." he said, and I ah'd, remembering what he'd told me yesterday.

We both leaned down to spit.

"I don't think we have time for a shower." I said, washing out my mouth and bustling to my closet. "Come on, we need to change."

"I don't have clothes with me." He said, and I nodded.

"I know that. Here." I tossed him one of my full sleeved t-shirts and jeans. "Wear those."

"Alright." he said, and removed his shirt.

"WOAH WOAH WOAH WOAH!" I shouted, covering my eyes and furiously turning the other way. "Go inside the bathroom, you fucking doofus!"

"We're both guys." he said, but he sounded teasing and I furiously tried to claw out my red cheeks with my fingers.

"Just- Just go in the freaking bathroom and change." I said, waiting for him to finish laughing and for the door to click shut.

I pouted to myself and grabbed some deodorant, spraying it after removing my clothes. I quickly changed, incase he just barged out. I wouldn't put it past him.

"Hey, can I come out?" he asked.

"Yes!" I threw the clothes I'd gone to sleep into my laundry basket. The jeans had dug into my skin, so I had these button shaped marks on my hips.

"Slight problem," I looked up and felt myself getting embarrassed again, seeing him in my clothes. "So like, these are a bit tight for me."

"..."

I stared at him, not understanding before it finally dawned onto me and my mouth fell open in a silent scream.

"N-Not possible!" I stuttered, marching over to him and grabbing his - my - t-shirt. "I'm bigger than you! It should fit just fine!"

"I guess I grew." Kile said, and grinned when I looked up to meet his eyes. "Also, I've always been slightly broader than you. It's not uncomfortable or anything though. So I'll wear it."

"Shit, this can't be true." I mumbled, feeling unusually inferior and small when we were this close. "I've always been bigger than you."

"Well, not anymore." he said, flicking my ear and walking past me to get his jacket and pack his clothes.

"Come, let's go down." I told him, also getting my jacket and opening the door. I lead the way downstairs, wincing when mum turned to me with a surprised expression.

"Rin? I thought you were staying back today." she said, getting up from the sofa.

"Right sorry. I overslept." I explained. "This is Kile, by the way."

"Hello, Mrs. Donatello. Thanks for letting me come over." Kile said, smiling widely and mum smiled too, walking to us.

"Hello, Kile. I saw you both sleeping last night when I came to call you down for dinner, but I didn't have the heart to wake either of you up." she confessed. "Come on, I'll fix some breakfast for you.

"Oh no that's fine!" Kile said, raising his hands up. "I've already overstayed my welcome."

"Nonsense. You're Rin's close friend right? Treat this as if it were your own home." Mum said, ruffling his hair before walking to the kitchen.

"Mum, we're going to miss first period." I complained, and she rolled her eyes.

"That's only first period. But you won't be able to pay attention the entire day without breakfast." she rebutted, rounding the island. "Anyways, it's all ready I just need to heat it up. I hope you don't mind avocado and toast, Kile."

"Sure, I love avocado." he said, sliding next to me to sit. "You really have a lovely house."

"He's super jealous." I added, and he elbowed me.

"Thank you. I designed it myself, actually." Mum laughed. "Feel free to drop by anytime, okay?"

"Sure." Kile said, and I waited impatiently for her to give the food.

"Mom, we're going to be really late!" I whined. "Can't you just pack it?"

"That's what I'm doing, you impatient cow." she rolled her eyes, and that's when I noticed the two paper bags in her hands. "I made them into sandwiches. Here you go."

Kile stared at his bag for a few moments, before carefully taking it. "This is for me?"

"Of course."

"I...Thank you. So much." I looked awkwardly at him, wondering why he was reacting that way when I remembered that his parents were hardly home, so he had to cook all by himself.

"Well, off you go. Be careful. Don't drive fast." She instructed, pushing us towards the door.

"Byeee." I called out, stepping out to the porch after grabbing my keys. Kile waved shyly to my mom, who smiled and waved back as we made our way to my car.

"Didn't you get your car too?" I asked, and Kile affirmed, gesturing to his car.

"I'll just take it back to school." Kile said, and I watched him go with slight regret as he opened the car door and slid in.

I lead the way because he was still unfamiliar with this part of town, leading us to the main road before glancing up periodically at the rear view mirror.

Every time I looked up, he did too, and our eyes would meet and he'd smile

I looked away, blushing slightly.

God, what was wrong with me? Ever since Evie had said those nonsensical things, all I could ever think about was that stupid idiot and got flustered at how affectionate he was. It wasn't fair, my brain was playing tricks on me, fooling me into getting embarrassed and shy around him.

When we reached school, I looked at the brown bag, debating on whether I should take it with me or just leave it here. I wasn't going to eat it anyways.

Deciding to take it, I got out of the car and jogged up to Kile, who was locking his car door.

"You didn't eat your breakfast?" he asked, and I shook my head.

"Want it?" I offered, and his eyes lit up before he nodded hungrily and grabbed it from me.

"These sandwiches are amazing." he said through a mouthful of bread, and I made a face before shoving him.

"Well eat fast because we're fucking late." I said, grabbing his arm and running up to the entrance. "What's your first class?"

"Comp, I think."

"Alright, then I'll see you later." I told him, waving as I stumbled up the stairs. He waved back before gulping the rest of the sandwich.

The teacher was pretty pissed that I was almost 40 minutes late to class, and sent me off with two extra work sheets to do, even though I thoroughly explained that I had diarrhoea and was stuck on the pot this morning. Insensitive jackass.

After class I was walking down the hallway when I suddenly felt a chill up my spine.

"Rin!" I heard Hale call out just a second before he crashed into me, sending us both toppling over. My heart dropped to my stomach for a second, but then I remembered that it was just Hale and we were in school.

"Why." I asked, fed up as he rolled us over and straddled me, grinning down at me.

"Guess what?!" he screamed, and I waited patiently for him to continue. "I got accepted into Ridgeway Uni!"

"Woah, holy shit!" I said, eyes going wide in shock as I gripped his forearms. "Seriously? Like seriously seriously?"

"Dude, seriously seriously seriously seriously!" he shrieked. "I don't believe an idiot like me got into Ridgeway!"

"I don't believe an idiot like you got into Ridgeway either!" I shrieked back.

Ridgeway University was one of the best Universities where we lived. It's super hard to get in for those who decide to write the exams. But to get in on recommendation, like Hale, is a spectacular feat.

"I'm so fucking proud of you." I said, and he laughed and leaned down to hug me tightly.

"What on earth?" I heard Donna say, and Hale was off of me in a second to go and barrel into here.

"I got into Ridgeway!"

"Ow- wait what?!"

"Hey, you okay?" I looked up to see Kile leaning over me, holding out a hand. He probably got here sometime in the commotion.

"Yep." I said, grabbing it and finding slightly insulted from the ease it took him to haul me up.

"Congratulations, Hale." Kile said kindly, and Hale turned to him.

"Thanks! It's literally my first choice! I'm so glad I got in." Hale sighed and physically deflated as he leaned down to rest on my shoulder. "Ah, now I can just wing finals."

"Guess we'll be attending college together." Kile smiled, and all three of us, Donna, Hale and I, turned to him simultaneously.

"What?"

"I got into Ridgeway too." he said. "I got accepted 2 months ago. I'm going there, already accepted."

"Fucking hell, of course you got early admission to the top college in the country." Hale snorted. "What are you going for?"

"I'm going for engineering, just a basic degree." Kile shrugged. "Have lots of options from there."

"I got in for Eco and math." Hale said. "Don, what about you?"

"Well, I've sent all my applications, and have heard back from a few. Not sure about the others though." Donna said.

"What are you going to do in college again?" I asked Donna.

"Oh, I want to attend a culinary academy." she answered.

"Hey where's Evie?" I asked, realising that she wasn't here yet.

"I don't think she came to school today." Donna said, looking around. "I didn't see her in chem."

"I wonder why she's absent?" Hale mused. "She usually messages if she does bunk."

"Maybe she's sick or something." Kile said. "And she's sleeping."

"Probably." Donna nodded.

I also agreed with them, but internally I couldn't help but worry about her.